A Hero of Our Time

Mikhail Lermontov

Translated by Hugh Aplin

ET REMOTISSIMA PROPE

Hesperus Classics

Hesperus Classics
Published by Hesperus Press Limited
4 Rickett Street, London SW6 1RU
www.hesperuspress.com

A Hero of Our Time first published in Russian in 1840
This translation first published by Hesperus Press Limited, 2005

Introduction and English language translation © Hugh Aplin, 2005
Foreword © Doris Lessing, 2005

Designed and typeset by Fraser Muggeridge
Printed in Italy by Graphic Studio Srl

ISBN: 1-84391-106-x

CONTENTS

When this novel appeared in Russia in 1840 there was shock, there was horror. It was a slander and a libel and a slur on the younger generation. This often happens when a novel or play touches to the quick, but we do have to admit to our appetite for shock and horror. The equivalent in our time was the Angry Young Men, and while the fuss and noise was largely the creation of the media, nevertheless it all went on for about ten years, and that couldn't have happened if people hadn't wanted to be shocked. There were actually reports of fathers trying to horsewhip their daughters' impudent suitors. Splendidly anachronistic stuff!

The emotions *A Hero of Our Time* evoked went rather deeper. Lermontov, unpleasantly attacked, said the book was indeed a portrait, not of himself, but of a generation. He was far from apologetic and spoke out of that sense of responsibility and authority then possessed by Russian writers. They saw themselves – and were generally regarded – as a public conscience. The writers of no other country have ever enjoyed such a role.

So when Lermontov said he had diagnosed the illness but it was not his business to prescribe the cure, he disappointed.

Now that the novel is set firmly in the perspective of the past, it takes its place as one in a gallery of similarly exemplary portraits, in a context of other novels, other heroes. Pechorin was a portrait not only of a certain type of Russian: the title fits well with heroes from other countries and even other times.

Byron is the best known of the dubious heroes; interesting that it is the author himself, not one of his characters, who typified scandalous youth. Byron's name blazed across Europe, and beyond.

It has been suggested that Byron, and Pechorin too, needed psychiatric treatment, but this view of them nullifies any glamour these heroes might have had. And they did, in plenty; both young women and men swooned over the *idea* of Byron. And, earlier, of Lovelace, the formidable opponent of Clarissa. Now Clarissa has come to the fore, but that tiresome and masochistic young woman – if anyone needed 'treatment', surely she did – was not what captivated then. No, it was Lovelace, certainly bad, probably mad – and everyone talked about him. There was closer and faster reciprocity in European literature then. Lovelace was one of Pechorin's progenitors. He certainly inspired Dostoevsky's Raskolnikov: his character and his ideas.

When Lovelace complained that a king might kill millions and be applauded for it, whereas if a private citizen did the same he would be punished, he could not know that the idea, and even the words, would echo for so long. Dostoevsky put almost the same words into Raskolnikov's mouth: to kill a horrible old woman must deserve a death sentence or exile, but battlefields of slain soldiers earn generals medals.

Since then generations of revolutionaries have claimed the idea as justification. Our terrorists are the natural children of Lovelace, Byron, Raskolnikov, Stavrogin and his gang of murderous anarchists. Whoever kills without a conscience has a long line of literary antecedents.

The disseminator of new or recycled slogans should be more aware of their power. When Bertolt Brecht said that to rob a bank was considered a crime but that to found one was the real crime, he could not have considered that the remark would turn whole populations into cheerful and conscienceless thieves justified to shoplift, empty hotels of anything they fancy, loot when they have the chance. 'Property is theft' is their defence.

'A Hero of Our Time' is the bitterest of titles. Perhaps we should be reminded what a hero is. When not so long ago terrorists killed an Italian he cried, 'I shall show you how an Italian can die.'

There it is, the hero, the authentic article. None of your ironic stances, the smiles at your own posturing. That cry could have – and probably did – resound over the battlefields of Troy.

Heroes of Pechorin's type abounded in Russia. Eugene Onegin, that unlikeable man, sullen and cold, was discussed as a symptom of the same disease. Soon would come Goncharov and Turgenev and the whole gamut of young men the critics would call superfluous. Then, later, came the critics spawned by communism, which reinvented the idea of hero, to whom the mere idea of self-doubt was impossible.

The construction of this clever novel enables us to see Grigory Alexandrovich Pechorin first as something not much worse than a poseur, and only later as one of the nastiest characters in fiction. Who could have any idea of his true nature in 'Bela', the first of the tales? In this there is much action, many daring deeds, affairs of honour, strenuous bravery, and so it is hard to understand that heroics are not his true nature but merely the convention of the time. In 'Bela' we see not much more than the young officer, in love and out of love, dashing, handsome. He says he has an unfortunate character, but whether it was the way he was brought up, or how he was made, he does not know. His soul was corrupted by society. Yes, he did love Bela, the Circassian beauty, but she bored him, just as the society ladies did. He strikes a modern note by saying he is to be pitied. 'Not my fault, but society's.'

The narrator claims it was not the French who started 'the fashion for being bored' but the English. Meaning who else but Byron…

Pechorin's girl, Bela, whom he has stolen from her family, is eventually killed, dying in a scene full of pathos. And Pechorin laughs. It is the excess of emotion he is laughing at – or protecting himself from. All this against backgrounds of splendid natural beauty.

So that is Pechorin as we first see him. If he had been killed then, in one of the heroic escapades he invited, we would have been left with this attitudinising young man: moody, handsome, brave. We may imagine him perhaps dining with Eugene Onegin who had turned up in some place far from society, having had to absent himself, since he too had killed someone he loved. If 'love' is a word we may use about either of them. They would certainly agree that none of it was their fault: they had been born out of their time.

It is in 'Princess Mary', the fourth piece and a part of Pechorin's journal, that his character is shown in its full nastiness: 'I sense in myself that insatiable greed which absorbs everything encountered on my way: I look at the sufferings and joys of others only in relation to myself, as nourishment that sustains my spiritual powers'; 'To be the cause of someone's suffering and joy, without having any positive right to be so – isn't that the sweetest nourishment for our pride?'; '…she'll spend a sleepless night crying'.

And an entry which is provocative indeed: 'I often wonder why I'm so persistent about winning the love of a young girl I don't want to seduce and will never marry? What's the point of this feminine coquetry?'

It is unlikely that an introspective anti-hero of our time would readily describe himself thus.

Because he did, it is instructive to imagine a woman behaving like Pechorin, blowing hot and cold, giving the come-on, then the cold shoulder, promising everything, then withdrawing herself and her smiles, becoming icy and indifferent. There would be no word bad enough for her. 'Flirt' and 'coquette' certainly: both words much worse then than now.

All this goes on in a spa town, full of fashionable people and officers, love affairs and intrigues. The scenery is spectacular. Pechorin commends it. He says the air is pure and fresh, like the kiss of a child. '…what more, one wonders, could you want?'

Among the visitors is a woman whom he has loved and left, now unhappily married. He makes sure to blow on the embers, but his target is the belle of the little town, whom all the men are after. It is her heart he is determined to break and we watch him doing it, fascinated, as we are by the cynical operators of *Les Liaisons dangereuses*.

This cruel torturer does exert fascination, and has done so for getting on for a hundred and seventy years.

Vladimir Nabokov once translated this novel, introducing it with a preface which puts into focus a good many troubling questions.

'…young Lermontov managed to create a fictional person whose romantic dash to cynicism, tigerlike suppleness and eagle eye, hot blood and cool head, tenderness and taciturnity, elegance and brutality, delicacy of perception and harsh passion to dominate, ruthlessness and awareness of it, are of lasting appeal to readers of all countries and centuries – especially to young readers.'

What we have here is a combination of the 'fictional person' as he might have appeared in a drawing room, all elegance and challenge, and the nasty truth of his journal, where his underside is spelt out for us.

I find Nabokov's evident admiration of Pechorin surprising. He was not one to spare his scorn – a commodity he had plenty of – for unpleasant behaviour, and we may be sure that if he had met Pechorin in life he would not have had much good to say about him.

So, then, life is one thing and literature another? To say that Jimmy Porter was a self-pitying crybaby who shocked the mature members of the first audiences, most of whom had had to endure the Second World War, is as irrelevant as to describe Pechorin as a bully and an emotional sadist?

Perhaps we have here one of literature's uses made plain. We may dream of a fictional person's 'romantic dash to cynicism, tigerlike suppleness and eagle eye', letting loose the tigers within us, or whine and whimper as much as we like, provided it is all kept safely on the page. God forbid that one should ever actually meet Pechorin (or Byron or Jimmy Porter).

Yet I – like, it seems, everyone else – have read this novel several times, young and old, always hooked, watching this ruthless young officer stroll through his life to its end, deservedly, in a duel… no, no, that was Lermontov.

Nabokov insists that Lermontov's claim that he was only describing a type was merely part of the artefact of the novel. It was evidently hard for Nabokov to commend 'young' Lermontov. His prose was bad, he said, he could not write, and his narrative full of inconsistencies. '…But the narrative surges on with such speed and force; such manly and romantic beauty pervades it; and the general purpose of Lermontov breathes such fierce integrity…'

Here is Vera, the woman with whom Pechorin shares a passionate past: ' "Tell me," she whispered eventually, "is it great fun for you tormenting me? I ought to hate you. Ever since we've known one another you've brought me nothing but suffering…" ' There follows an ardent and rapturous kiss. And so forth. (That *and so forth* was certainly suggested to me by the ghost of Pechorin.)

Generations of women have wondered if they would have made fools of themselves over Byron, Lovelace, Pechorin. Here is the probable truth of the matter, in Vera's whisper.

We do have to admit that there are women who cannot resist the emotional brigand.

– Doris Lessing, 2005

Note:

The quotations by Vladimir Nabokov are taken from *A Hero of Our Time* by Mikhail Lermontov, translated by Vladimir Nabokov in collaboration with Dmitri Nabokov. Foreword by Vladimir Nabokov (Oxford: Oxford University Press, 1984).

The three works in this volume represent all the prose fiction that Mikhail Lermontov composed using the mountains of the Caucasus as a backdrop. In fact, with the exception of the brief 'Panorama of Moscow', written at the age of about nineteen, these were the only works in prose that he ever completed. Just one of them, *A Hero of Our Time*, was published in the writer's lifetime, and it is the only one that is widely known today. The physiological sketch 'A Caucasian' was specially written in 1840 or 1841 for a collection of works all of a similar type by a number of authors and entitled *Our People, Drawn from Life by Russians*; the work found disfavour with the censor, however, and was withdrawn. The status of 'Ashik-Kerib' is more obscure: it appears to be an unrevised transcription from 1837 of a folktale well known in slightly differing versions throughout the Caucasus on which Lermontov may or may not have intended to do further work. It could be argued that these two shorter pieces have little more than curiosity value today. But like his many poetic works (also of varying length and literary value) that were influenced by the landscapes and traditions of the Caucasus, they help testify alongside his novel to the substantial part the region played in forming the creative consciousness of one of the earliest of Russia's great novelists.

There can be no doubt that *A Hero of Our Time* is a masterpiece, and the translator who takes on any classic text sets himself the challenge of doing justice to a major cultural phenomenon. Yet in tackling *A Hero of Our Time* the translator is faced with a double challenge. Not only does he have before him Lermontov's beguilingly straightforward, yet wonderfully complex novel, but also at his back is the shadow of another titan of Russian literature, Vladimir Nabokov. Nabokov made his own translation of *A Hero of Our Time* in the 1950s, and in his foreword was utterly scathing about the quality of all previous attempts to render the novel into English. His basic complaint, probably not lacking in justification, was that the authors of earlier versions had been too concerned with producing prose that read well in English, irrespective of its accuracy in reflecting the original Russian. And it is hard to imagine that he would have been any more generous about the very few new translations of the novel that have appeared since his own.

Nabokov was surely right to demand of the translator absolute fidelity to the linguistic and stylistic quirks of his source text. Yet his contention that a translation must, of necessity, be recognisable as such if it is to have pretensions to exactitude is more debatable. As well as dealing with the individual words, the translator must attempt to reproduce the overall stylistic feel of the original, a quality sometimes not easily defined, yet certainly accessible to the sensitive reader. And if that feel is of effortless elegance, as is often the case in, say, Turgenev, then the 'smoothness' that Nabokov so berates is precisely what the translator should seek to achieve. Too pedantic an approach can result in a translation being all but unreadable – as is the case at times with Nabokov's version of Pushkin's *Eugene Onegin*, itself a work of magical linguistic lightness.

This establishment of principles seems appropriate because *A Hero of Our Time* is a work in which exploration of language, story-telling and interpretation (a variant of translation, translation of meaning) is central to the author's purpose. The novel's very first episode exemplifies this concern, when the narrator's mystification about his vehicle's slow rate of progress is shown to stem from his inability to understand what is being shouted at the bullocks that are pulling it. Indeed, throughout the first story, 'Bela', one has a sense of disorientation; the narrator is, after all, a travel writer, forever confronting unfamiliar scenes in a land full of incomprehensible languages. It is in theory the alien nature of what he describes for his readers that gives his writing its interest.

Equally full of mysteries is the first of the stories taken from the journal of the hero, Pechorin, himself. Here, too, the reader meets with a traveller who is confronted with a foreign language in an unfamiliar place and who remains in the dark, both literally and metaphorically, almost throughout the story. It is most appropriate that the name of the little town of Taman is so like such Russian words as *temen* ('darkness') and *tuman* ('fog') – phenomena which obscure our view of the world around us.

Wordplay is itself a recurring feature of the novel, and not only in the verbal duelling that makes 'Princess Mary' such a delight to read. Take, for example, the names of various characters: Vulic, the wilful Serb in 'The Fatalist', seems as much linked to the French *vouloir* as is the beautiful Bela to the French *belle*. And yet we are warned in 'Princess Mary' that names can be deceptive – Werner is Russian despite his German-sounding name; on the other hand he is true to the meaning of the Russian homonym *verno*, for he behaves both 'loyally' and 'reliably'. And Mary herself is perfectly Russian, a fashion for things foreign being the reason for the Anglicisation of her name. But the reader should have been aware from a very early stage of the danger of misinterpreting labels: the travel writer takes great pains in 'Bela' to explain the true origin of the name of the Chertova Valley. This is a passage that may seem a mere naturalistic digression from the gripping story of Bela and Pechorin, but it is actually one of a number of reminders about how to approach what is ultimately the aim of most readers of the book – gaining an understanding of Pechorin, the hero.

The title of the novel caused a great deal of controversy when it first appeared in 1840, and this prompted Lermontov to respond with his foreword to the second edition when it came out in the following year. Pechorin's entitlement to the status of hero had immediately been called into question, and his creator felt obliged to shed the multiple masks behind which he had concealed himself in the novel to intervene with an explanation of his intent. (It should be stressed that this foreword is the only section of the book that can be considered as written from the point of view of the author: thereafter we hear only the voices of his creations, the travel writer, Pechorin and, briefly in letters, Vera and Werner; all other voices – even that of Maxim Maximych, the source for most of the story 'Bela' – are filtered through the travel writer and Pechorin.) Without once using the word 'irony', but not without liberal use of irony itself, Lermontov warns against too literal an interpretation of words. Pechorin is, perhaps, a typical literary hero of his time, and may be a figure typical of Russian society of his time, but he is not necessarily being offered as an exemplar for the reading public.

The sophisticated modern reader, well acquainted with anti-heroes, is unlikely to be confused for long about Pechorin's position in relation to virtue and vice. But that does not mean he is an unattractive character – young readers in particular, in Russia and beyond, continue to come under his spell and respond to him in a way that Lermontov might not have commended. Nor is he an uncontroversial character, for literary historians, like the critics of the 1840s, have long been divided in their interpretation of Pechorin, depending on whether they have seen him as the victim of a repressive age and regime or the product of an immoral philosophy of life. It is one of the novel's enduring strengths that it can give rise to a great variety of readings, and much of the ambiguity achieved derives from Lermontov's exploitation of varying points of view in the novel, further enhanced by its unusual structure.

Our first impressions of Pechorin come from Maxim Maximych, a man who knew him several years before and understood him but little. His narrative is passed on by the travel writer, a professional author who freely admits to altering his material (in the note to Kazbich's song). We next see Pechorin through the eyes of the travel writer himself; but the latter, as he admits when describing him, is already predisposed to interpret Pechorin in a particular way. This story also underlines what an unreliable narrator Maxim Maximych is, from his exaggeration of his closeness to Pechorin to his claims to abstention from alcohol. Finally we are presented with Pechorin's own visions of himself, prefaced by the travel writer's encouragement to take them at face value, since they were not intended for an audience. But it is interesting to note here that in a manuscript variant of this foreword its author wrote:

I have looked through Pechorin's notes and remarked from several places that he was preparing them for publication... In fact, in several places Pechorin addresses his readers...

This comment might have gone some way to explaining the differences between on the one hand 'Taman' and 'The Fatalist', with their feel of the rounded story, and on the other 'Princess Mary', with its sense of immediacy and unfolding events. But its excision made it easier for the reader to be encouraged to believe, and thus to sympathise with Pechorin. The hero is actually another untrustworthy, highly manipulative narrator, whose occasional sincerity is laced with blatant self-delusion, yet with whom we may want to side, despite his arrogance and egotism, thanks to his confidential, intimate tone and his privileged position in the narrative: Grushnitsky, for example, appears foolish precisely because Pechorin presents him as such.

In theory, then, the reader moves ever closer to Pechorin as he journeys through the book and should be able to come to an increasingly clear understanding of the hero. In practice, however, the misunderstandings and assumptions of the naive early narrators are replaced by the evasions and obfuscations of the disingenuous Pechorin. The reintroduction of Maxim Maximych on the novel's final page, harking back to the opening story, serves to reinforce the notion that one has merely circled around Pechorin. He remains an enigma.

Nabokov suggested that the five stories forming the bulk of the novel are like five mountain peaks along a Caucasian mountain road. Perhaps a better analogy is provided by Lermontov himself when he has the narrator of 'Bela' describe his inelegant entry into a hut that provides refuge from a storm: three slippery steps and two dark rooms filled with smoke and a variety of animal noises are a splendid metaphor for this endlessly engaging novel.

– Hugh Aplin, 2005

A Hero of Our Time

In any book the foreword is the first and, at the same time, the last thing; it serves either as an explanation of the writer's aim, or as a justification and response to criticism. But readers are not normally concerned with the moral aim or with attacks in journals, and thus they do not read forewords. Yet it is a pity that this is the case, especially in our country. Our public is still so young and ingenuous that it does not understand a fable if it does not find a moral at the end of it. It does not get a joke, does not sense an irony; it is simply badly brought up. It does not yet know that in decent society and in a decent book blatant abuse can have no place; that the modern level of education has invented a tool more sharp, almost invisible and nonetheless deadly, which, dressed up as flattery, strikes an irresistible and sure blow. Our public resembles a man from the provinces who, if overhearing a conversation between two diplomats belonging to hostile courts, would remain certain that each of them was deceiving his own government in favour of the tenderest mutual friendship.

This book experienced for itself quite recently the unfortunate trust of some readers, and even journals, in the literal meaning of words. Some were dreadfully offended, and genuinely so, that they were being offered as an example such an immoral man as the 'Hero of Our Time'; while others remarked very astutely that the writer had drawn his own portrait and the portraits of his acquaintances... An old and sorry joke! But evidently Rus is made in such a way that everything in it gets updated apart from absurdities like that. In our country the most magical of magical fairy tales can barely avoid reproach for attempting an attack on someone's character!

The 'Hero of Our Time', my dear sirs, is indeed a portrait, but not of a single man: it is a portrait compiled from the vices of our entire generation in their full development. Again you will say to me that a man cannot be so bad, but I shall say to you that if you have believed in the possible existence of all those tragic and romantic villains, why ever do you not give credence to the reality of Pechorin? If you have revelled in fantasies much more awful and ugly, why ever does this character, even as a fantasy, find no mercy within you? Is it not simply because there is more truth in him than you would wish?…

Will you say that morality does not gain from it? Forgive me. People have been fed on sweetmeats quite enough; it has ruined their stomachs: bitter medicines are needed, caustic truths. But do not think after this, however, that the author of this book ever had the arrogant dream of becoming a corrector of human vices. God preserve him from such ignorance! He simply found it amusing to draw modern man as he understands him, and has - to his and your misfortune - too often encountered him. Let it suffice that the disease has been pointed out, but how it is to be cured - that God alone knows!

I

Bela

I was travelling by post-chaise from Tiflis[1]. The entire load of my chaise consisted of one small valise, which was crammed half full of travel notes about Georgia. The greater part of them, luckily for you, is lost, but the valise with the remaining things, luckily for me, has remained intact.

The sun was already beginning to hide behind a snowy crest when I entered the Koyshaur Valley. The Ossetian driver urged the horses on indefatigably so as to be in time to ascend Mount Koyshaur before nightfall, and was singing songs at the top of his voice. A glorious place is that valley! On all sides unassailable mountains, reddish cliffs draped in green ivy and crowned with groups of plane trees, yellow precipices criss-crossed with gullies, while way up high is the golden fringe of the snows, and down below the silver thread of the Aragva, entwined with another nameless little river that bursts noisily out from a black, mist-filled gorge, stretches out and glistens like the scaly skin of a snake.

On arriving at the foot of Mount Koyshaur we stopped by an inn. Here there was a noisy crowd of a couple of dozen Georgians and mountain tribesmen; nearby a caravan of camels had stopped for the night. I had to hire bullocks to pull my chaise up this damned mountain because it was already autumn and there was black ice about – and the mountain is a climb of about two kilometres.

There was nothing for it; I hired six bullocks and several Ossetians. One of them hoisted my valise onto his shoulders, the others started helping the bullocks with little more than their shouting.

Behind my chaise a team of four bullocks was pulling another chaise as though there were nothing to it, despite the fact that it was loaded up high. This fact surprised me. Behind it walked its master, taking the occasional puff at a little Kabardian pipe decorated in silver. He was wearing an officer's frock coat without epaulettes and a shaggy Circassian hat. He seemed about fifty years old; the swarthy colouring of his face showed it was long acquainted with the Transcaucasian sun, and his prematurely grey whiskers did not correspond to his firm walk and cheerful look. I went up to him and bowed; he returned my bow in silence and let out a huge puff of smoke.

'We seem to be travelling the same way?'

He again bowed in silence.

'You're probably going to Stavropol?'

'Yes, sir… with Government belongings.'

'Please tell me why this heavy chaise of yours is being pulled easily by four bullocks, while six beasts with the help of all these Ossetians can scarcely budge my empty one?'

He gave a sly smile and glanced at me meaningfully.

'You're probably not long in the Caucasus?'

'About a year,' I replied.

He gave a second smile.

'What of it?'

'Oh, nothing, sir! These Asiatics are terrible rogues! You think they're helping by shouting? But who the devil can make out what it is they're shouting? Yet the bullocks understand them; harness up as many as twenty, but if they shout something their own special way, the bullocks won't so much as move… Terrible rogues! But what can you do with them?… They love fleecing travellers… The rascals have been spoiled! You'll see, they'll have a tip out of you as well. But I know them, they won't con me!'

'So have you served here long?'

'Yes, I was already serving here in Alexei Petrovich's* time,' he replied, assuming a dignified air. 'When he arrived at the Line[3] I was a second lieutenant,' he added, 'and under him I was given two promotions for action against the mountain tribesmen.'

'And now you're?…'

'Now I'm in the Third Line Battalion. And yourself, might I make so bold as to enquire?…'

I told him.

With this the conversation ceased and we continued to walk alongside one another in silence. On the mountain summit we found snow. The sun set, and night followed day without an interval, as is normally the way in the south; but thanks to the light coming from

* Ermolov[2]

the snows we were easily able to make out the road, which was still climbing, albeit not so steeply now. I ordered my valise to be put in the chaise, the bullocks to be replaced with horses, and for the last time looked back at the valley – but the dense mist rolling in waves out of the gorges had covered it completely, and no longer did a single sound reach our ears from there. The Ossetians surrounded me noisily and demanded a tip; but the staff captain yelled at them so threateningly that they scattered in a flash.

'That's the sort of people they are!' he said. 'They don't even know how to say "bread" in Russian, but they've learnt, "Officer, give money for vodka!" The Tatars are certainly better, in my view: at least they don't drink…'

There remained about a kilometre to the posting station. It was quiet all around, so quiet that the flight of a mosquito could be followed by its buzzing. To the left was the blackness of a deep gorge; beyond it and in front of us the dark blue mountain summits, creased with wrinkles and covered with layers of snow, were outlined against the pale horizon that still retained the final glow of the sunset. Stars were beginning to glimmer in the dark sky, and, strangely, it seemed to me that they were much higher than in our northern parts. On either side of the road bare, black rocks jutted up; bushes peeped out from beneath the snow in places, but not a single dry leaf was stirring, and it was pleasant to hear amidst this – nature's sleep of the dead – the snorting of the three tired post-horses and the irregular tinkling of the Russian harness bell.

'The weather will be glorious tomorrow!' I said. The staff captain said not a word in reply, but pointed out to me a high mountain rising up directly opposite us.

'What's that?' I asked.

'Mount Gud.'

'Well, so what?'

'Look how it's steaming.'

And indeed, Mount Gud was steaming; over its flanks crawled light streams of vapour, while on its summit lay a black storm cloud, so black that it seemed like a stain on the dark sky.

We could already make out the posting station, the roofs of the huts surrounding it, and before us glimmered welcoming lights, when there was a gust of damp, cold wind, the gorge set up a droning noise, and light rain began to fall. I had scarcely managed to throw on my Caucasian felt cloak before the snow started coming down. I looked at the staff captain with reverence...

'We'll have to spend the night here,' he said in annoyance: 'you won't get across the mountains in a snowstorm like this. Well? Have there been any avalanches on the Krestovaya?' he asked the driver.

'No, mister,' replied the Ossetian driver: 'but there's a lot hanging, a lot.'

Since there were no rooms for travellers at the posting station, we were allocated a place for the night in a smoky hut. I invited my travelling companion to join me in a glass of tea, for I had a cast-iron kettle with me – my sole comfort in my travels through the Caucasus.

One side of the hut was stuck right up against a cliff; three slippery, wet steps led to its door. I groped my way in and stumbled upon a cow (amongst these people the cattle shed takes the place of the servants' hall). I did not know where to turn: there were sheep bleating here, a dog growling there. Fortunately, over to one side a dim light flashed and helped me to find another opening with a resemblance to a door. Here there was revealed quite a diverting picture: a broad hut, the roof of which rested on two smoke-blackened pillars, was full of people. In the middle crackled a small fire, made up on the ground, and the smoke, pushed back from an opening in the roof by the wind, was spreading all around in such a thick shroud that for a long time I could not get my bearings. By the fire sat two old women, a host of children and one lean Georgian, all dressed in rags. There was nothing for it, we took shelter by the fire, got our pipes going, and soon the kettle began to hiss affably.

'Pitiable people!' I said to the staff captain, indicating our dirty hosts, who were silently looking at us in a sort of stupefaction.

'They're a really dim lot!' he replied. 'Would you believe it? They don't know how to do anything, they're not capable of any education! Our Kabardians or Chechens, although they may be villains and paupers, at least they're madcaps at the same time, whereas this lot don't even have any love of weapons: you won't see a decent dagger on a single one of them. They're real Ossetians!'

'And were you in Chechnya long?'

'Yes, I was stationed with my company in a fort there for about ten years, near Kamenny Brod – do you know it?'

'I've heard of it.'

'Yes, old chap, those cut-throats got on our nerves; they're quieter nowadays, thank God, but it used to be the case that if you went a hundred paces outside the ramparts, a hairy devil would be sitting there on watch somewhere or other: no sooner had you let your mind wander, before you knew it – either a lasso round your neck or a bullet in the back of the head. But they're fine fellows!…'

'And I expect you've had a lot of adventures?' I said, spurred on by curiosity.

'Of course I have! I have…'

Here he began tweaking his left whisker, hung his head and fell into thought. I was terribly keen to drag a little story of some sort out of him – a desire characteristic of all who travel and write. In the meantime the tea finished brewing; I pulled two travelling glasses out of my valise, poured the tea and set one glass before him. He took a sip and, as though to himself, said: 'Yes, I have!' This exclamation gave me great hopes. I know old Caucasian types like having a bit of a chat, telling a tale or two; they get to do it so rarely: one of them might be stationed for five years or so somewhere in the sticks with his company, and for the entire five years no one will say 'Good day' to him (because the sergeant-major wishes him, 'Good day, sir'). Yet there would be plenty of things to chat about: wild, curious people all around; every day danger, marvellous incidents taking place, and then you have to feel sorry that so little gets written down in our country.

'Would you like to lace it with some rum?' I said to my companion. 'I've got some white rum from Tiflis; it's cold now.'

'No, sir, thanking you kindly. I don't drink.'

'Why's that?'

'Just because. I made a pledge to myself. Once when I was still a second lieutenant, you know – we took a drop too much among ourselves, and during the night there was an alarm; and so we turned out before the soldiers a bit tipsy, and we really caught it when Alexei Petrovich found out: my goodness, how angry he was! Very nearly had us court-martialled. That's the way of it, you can live for a whole year

9

sometimes without seeing anyone, and if you've got vodka there too – you're a goner!'

On hearing this I almost lost hope.

'Take the Circassians even,' he continued: 'no sooner do they have a skinful of bouza⁴ at a wedding or a funeral than the fighting starts. I once barely got away with my life, even though I was the guest of a friendly prince.'

'However did that happen?'

'Well,' – he filled up his pipe, drew on it, and began to tell the tale – 'well, you see, I was stationed with my company in a fort beyond the Terek at the time – it'll soon be five years since. One day in the autumn a transport arrived with provisions: in the transport was an officer, a young man of about twenty-five. He reported to me in full uniform and announced that he'd been ordered to remain with me in the fort. He was so slim and white, the tunic he was wearing was so nice and new that I guessed straight away he'd not been with us in the Caucasus long. "I suppose," I asked him, "you've been transferred here from Russia?" – "Yes, sir, Staff Captain, sir," he replied. I took him by the hand and said: "Delighted, delighted. You'll find it a bit dull… but well, we'll live as friends, you and I. And please, do just call me Maxim Maximych, and please – why this full uniform? Wear your cap whenever you come and see me." He was assigned quarters and he settled down in the fort.'

'And what was his name?' I asked Maxim Maximych.

'His name was… Grigory Alexandrovich *Pechorin*. He was a splendid fellow, I'll make so bold as to assure you – only a bit strange. I mean, for example, in the rain, in the cold, hunting all day long; everyone'll be frozen through, tired – but he's all right. Yet another time he's sitting in his room, there'll be a puff of wind and he claims he's caught a cold; a shutter'll bang, he'll jump and turn pale; yet I've seen him going for a wild boar one on one; there were times you wouldn't get a word out of him for hours on end, but then sometimes when he started telling stories, you'd just split your sides laughing… Yes, sir, there were some very strange things about him, and he must be a rich man: he had such a lot of expensive bits and pieces!…'

'And did he stay with you long?' I continued questioning.

'About a year. But then it's a year to remember all the same; he caused me a lot of trouble, but I don't think badly of him! After all, some people really do have it written in their stars that lots of unusual things are to happen to them!'

'Unusual?' I exclaimed with an inquisitive look, pouring him some more tea.

'Well, I'll tell you about it. Around six kilometres from the fort there lived a friendly prince. His young son, a boy of fifteen or so, took to riding out to visit us: it used to be every day, first one thing, then another. And we certainly spoilt him, we did, Grigory Alexandrovich and I. And what a cut-throat he was, a dab hand at anything you could name, whether it was picking up a hat at full tilt or shooting a gun. This is the one bad thing about him: he had a terrible weakness for money. Once, for a laugh, Grigory Alexandrovich promised to give him a gold piece if he'd steal the best goat from his father's herd for him; and what do you think? The very next night he dragged it in by the horns. And there were times we took it into our heads to tease him, and his eyes would get all bloodshot, and his hand would go straight to his dagger. "Hey, Azamat, it'll cost you dear," I'd say to him: "you'll end up losing your head!"

'One day the old prince himself comes to invite us to a wedding: he was marrying off his elder daughter, and he and I were *kunaky*[5]: so, you know, you just can't refuse, even if he is a Tatar. We set off. In the village a whole host of dogs greeted us with their noisy barking. The women, when they caught sight of us, hid themselves; those whose faces we could get a look at were far from beauties. "I had a much better opinion of Circassian girls," Grigory Alexandrovich said to me. "Hang on!" I answered with a grin. I had something in mind.

'In the prince's hut a whole host of people had already gathered. Asiatics, you know, are in the habit of inviting the world and his wife to a wedding. We were received with all honours and led into the private rooms. Still, I'd not forgotten to take good note of where they'd put our horses – you know, in case of anything unforeseen.'

'And how do they celebrate a wedding?' I asked the staff captain.

'Just ordinarily. First of all a mullah will read them something from the Koran; then presents are given to the young couple and all their relatives; they eat, drink bouza; then begins the display of

11

horsemanship, and there's always some ragamuffin or other, all soiled, and on a lousy, lame little horse, who plays up, clowns about, gets the entire gang laughing; then, when it gets dark, in the private rooms there begins, to put it our way, a ball. A poor little old man strums away on a three-stringed… I've forgotten what they call it… well, like our balalaika. The lasses and the young lads get into two files opposite one another, clap their hands and sing. Then one of the lasses and one man come out into the centre and begin reciting verses to each other in a sing-song way, anything at all, and the rest join in all together. Pechorin and I were sitting in the place of honour, and up to him came the host's younger daughter, a girl of sixteen or so, and sang him… how can I put it?… a sort of compliment.'

'Whatever was it she sang, do you remember?'

'Yes, I think it went like this:

"Elegant are our young horsemen, and the kaftans they wear are covered in silver, but the young Russian officer is more elegant than they, and the galloons he wears are golden. He is like a poplar among them, but he cannot grow, he cannot blossom in our garden."

Pechorin got up, bowed to her, putting his hand on his forehead and then his heart, and asked me to reply to her; I know their language well and translated his reply.

'When she moved away from us, I whispered to Grigory Alexandrovich: "Well, then, how about her?"'

'"Delightful!" he replied. "But what's her name?" – "Her name's Bela," I replied.

'And she certainly was a looker: tall, slim, black eyes, like a mountain chamois's, that really gazed into your soul. Pechorin was deep in thought and didn't take his eyes off her, and she shot quite frequent looks at him from under her brows. But Pechorin wasn't alone in admiring the pretty Princess: from the corner of the room another pair of eyes was watching her, fixed, fiery. I started looking closely and recognised my old acquaintance Kazbich. He was, you know, not exactly friendly, not exactly unfriendly. There were a lot of suspicions about him, although he'd not been found out in any mischief. He'd sometimes bring sheep to us in the fort and sell them cheaply, only he never bargained: pay up what he asked – try what you like, he wouldn't reduce the price. They used to say of him that he liked hanging around with the outlaws over the Kuban River, and, to tell the truth, he really did have the look of a scoundrel: he was small, dry, broad-shouldered... And cunning, he was cunning as a devil! His coat was always ripped, covered in patches, but his weapons were covered in silver. And his horse was famous throughout Kabarda – and you certainly couldn't imagine anything better than that horse. There was good reason for all horsemen to envy him, and more than once people tried to steal the horse, only they didn't succeed. It's as if I could see that horse now: black as pitch, legs like strings and eyes the equal of Bela's; and what strength! Gallop as much as fifty kilometres; and trained – ran after its master like a dog, even knew his voice! He never even used to tether it. What a horse for a brigand!...

'That evening Kazbich was more sullen than ever, and I noticed he had a mail shirt on under his coat. "He's not wearing that mail shirt for nothing," I thought: "he's got to be planning something."

'It grew stuffy in the hut and I went out to freshen up in the open air. Night was already coming down on the mountains and mist was beginning to roam through the gorges.

'I took it into my head to turn under the shelter where our horses were, so as to see if they had any fodder, and besides, better safe than sorry: I had a splendid horse after all, and more than one Kabardian had given it loving looks, repeating: *yakshi tkhe, chek yakshi*[6] all the time!

'I'm stealing along beside the fence and suddenly I hear voices; I recognised one voice straight away: it was that scamp Azamat, our host's son; the other spoke more rarely and more quietly. "What are they discussing here?" I thought: "Not my horse, is it?" So I squatted down by the fence and began listening intently, trying not to miss a single word. At times the noise of songs and the chatter of voices coming out on the air from the hut drowned a conversation I found curious.

' "You have a splendid horse!" said Azamat. "If I were the master of the house and had a herd of three hundred mares, I would give half of them in exchange for your steed, Kazbich!"

' "Ah, Kazbich!" I thought, and remembered the mail shirt.

' "Yes," answered Kazbich, after some silence: "in the whole of Kabarda you will not find another like him. Once – it was on the other side of the Terek – I was riding with some outlaws to try and drive away the Russians' herds of horses; we did not have good fortune and we split up, all going in different directions. Four Cossacks were racing after me; I could already hear the cries of the giaours behind me, and in front of me was thick forest. I lay low in the saddle, entrusted myself to Allah, and for the first time in my life I insulted my horse with a blow of the whip. Like a bird he dived between the branches; sharp thorns tore my clothes, dry elm branches hit me across the face. My mount jumped across tree stumps, bursting through bushes with his chest. I would have done better to abandon him at the forest's edge and disappear in the trees on foot, but I felt sorry to part with him – and the Prophet rewarded me. Several shots whistled over my head; already I could hear the hastening Cossacks racing in my wake… Suddenly there was a deep trench in front of me; my steed thought for a moment – then jumped. His hind hooves fell from the opposite edge and he hung on his forelegs. I dropped the reins and flew into the gully; that saved my mount: he leapt out. The Cossacks saw it all, but not one of them came down to look for me: they probably thought I had been fatally injured, and I heard them rushing to catch my mount. My heart was bleeding; I crawled along the gully through dense grass; I take a look: the forest has come to an end, several Cossacks are riding out of it into a clearing, and then my Karagyoz leaps out of it straight towards them; shouting, they all dashed after him; they chased after him for a long, long time, and one in particular very nearly threw a lasso around his neck a couple of times. I began to tremble, lowered my eyes and started praying. A few moments later I raise them and see my Karagyoz is flying, his tail streaming out, free as the wind, while far behind, one after another, the giaours are strung out across the steppe on their exhausted mounts. It is the truth, by Allah, the honest truth! Late into the night I sat in my gully. Suddenly, what do you think, Azamat? In the gloom I hear a mount running about on the edge of the gully, snorting, neighing and beating its hooves on the ground; I recognised the voice of my Karagyoz: it was him, my comrade!… Since that time we have not been apart."

'And I could hear him running his hand down his steed's smooth neck, calling it various tender names.

' "If I had a herd of a thousand mares," said Azamat, "I would give it all to you in exchange for your Karagyoz."

' "*Yok*,[7] I do not want them," replied Kazbich indifferently.

' "Listen, Kazbich," said Azamat, coaxing him: "you are a good man, you are a courageous horseman, but my father is afraid of the Russians and does not allow me into the mountains; give me your horse, and I shall do anything you want, steal for you from my father his best rifle or sabre, whatever you might desire – and his sabre is a genuine *gurda*[8]: put the blade against your hand, it will bite into the body by itself; and a shirt of mail like yours is nothing."

'Kazbich was silent.

' "The first time I saw your mount," continued Azamat: "when he was whirling and jumping beneath you, flaring his nostrils, and the sparks from flints were flying from under his hooves, something incomprehensible happened in my soul, and since then everything has grown wearisome to me: I have looked with scorn upon my father's best steeds, I have felt ashamed to be seen on them, and anguish has taken hold of me; and, in anguish, I have spent days on end sitting on a crag, and at every moment your black steed has appeared in my thoughts with his elegant stride, with his smooth back, straight as an arrow; he has looked me in the eyes with his bold gaze as though he wanted to say something. I shall die, Kazbich, if you do not sell him to me!" said Azamat in a quavering voice.

'I heard him start crying: I should mention to you that Azamat was a very stubborn boy, and there was no way you could get any tears out of him, even when he was rather younger.

'In reply to his tears I heard something like laughter.

' "Listen!" said Azamat in a firm voice: "You see, I am ready to do anything. Do you want me to steal my sister for you? How she dances! How she sings! And her gold embroidery is a wonder! Even the Turkish Padishah never had such a wife… Do you want me to? Wait for me tomorrow night there in the gorge where the torrent races: I shall go by with her to the neighbouring village – and she is yours. Surely Bela is worth your steed?"

'Kazbich was silent for a long, long time; finally, instead of replying, he struck up an old song in a low voice:[*]

> "*Many the beauties that live in our hills,*
> *Stars are ablaze in the dusk of their eyes.*
> *Loving them's sweet and a fate to be envied*
> *But better by far is a young man's freedom.*
> *Gold may well purchase you three or four wives,*
> *But there's no price for a steed bold and true:*
> *He'll chase the wind through the steppe and not falter,*
> *Will not betray you, will not deceive you.*" [9]

'In vain did Azamat beg him to agree, and he cried, and he flattered him, and he made vows; finally Kazbich cut him short impatiently:

' "Go away, you crazy little boy! How are you to ride my mount? He will throw you off in the first three paces and you will crack your head open on the rocks."

' "Me!" shouted Azamat in fury, and the iron of a child's dagger rang out on a mail shirt. A strong hand pushed him off, and the way he hit the wattle fence set the fence swaying. "There's going to be some fun!" I thought. I dashed into the stable, bridled our horses and led them out to the yard at the rear. Two minutes later there was already a terrible rumpus inside the hut. This is what happened. Azamat ran in there with his coat ripped, saying Kazbich had tried to knife him. Everyone leapt outside, grabbed their guns – and the fun began! Shouting, noise, shots; only Kazbich was already mounted and spinning down the street like a devil in the midst of the crowd, fending everyone off with his sabre.

"It's no good paying the price for another man's indiscretions," I said to Grigory Alexandrovich, catching him by the arm: "hadn't we better get out of here quickly?"

' "Let's wait and see how it ends."

' "It'll end badly for sure; it's always the way with these Asiatics: they've downed enough bouza, so now the carnage has begun!" – We mounted up and galloped off home.'

[*] I beg the forgiveness of readers for putting Kazbich's song into verse, when it was communicated to me – it goes without saying – in prose; but habit is second nature.

16

'And what about Kazbich?' I asked the staff captain impatiently.

'What can happen to men like that!' he replied, finishing his glass of tea. 'He slipped away, of course!'

'And unhurt?' I asked.

'God knows! They're hardy, brigands! I, sir, have seen some in action, for example: I mean, all full of bayonet-holes, he is, like a sieve, but keeps on brandishing a sabre.'

After some silence the staff captain continued, stamping his foot on the ground:

'There's one thing I'll never forgive myself: I don't know what possessed me, but on arriving at the fort I told Grigory Alexandrovich all I'd heard while sitting behind the fence; he laughed – he was a cunning one! – and had an idea himself.'

'And what was that? Please tell me.'

'Well, there's nothing for it! I've started the story, so I've got to continue.

'After about four days Azamat arrives at the fort. As usual he dropped in on Grigory Alexandrovich, who was always feeding him delicacies. I was there. A conversation started about horses, and Pechorin began singing the praises of Kazbich's horse: it's just so spirited, beautiful, like a chamois – well, simply, according to him, there's not one like it in all the world.

'The young Tatar's little eyes began to glitter, but it was as if Pechorin didn't notice; I'd start talking about something else, but immediately, just look at that, he'd turn the conversation back to Kazbich's horse. It was the same story every time Azamat came. Three weeks or so later I started to notice that Azamat was getting pale and pining, as they do in novels, sir, on account of love. Wasn't that extraordinary?...

'You see, it was later I found out the whole of the caper: Grigory Alexandrovich had teased him so much, he was ready to drown himself. Once he went and said to him: "I can see that horse has really taken your fancy, Azamat; but you're as likely to clap eyes on it as you are on the back of your own head! Well, tell me, what would you give the man who presented you with it as a gift?..."

' "Anything he wanted," replied Azamat.

' "In that case, I'll get it for you, only on one condition… Swear you'll fulfil it…"

' "I swear… You swear too!"

' "Very well! I swear the mount will be in your possession; only in exchange for it you must give me your sister Bela: Karagyoz will be her bride-money. I hope the trade will be advantageous for you."

'Azamat was silent.

' "You don't want to? Well, as you wish! I thought you were a man, but you're still a child: it's too soon for you to be riding horses…"

'Azamat flared up. "What about my father?" he said.

' "Doesn't he ever go away?"

' "That's true…"

' "Agreed?…"

' "Agreed," whispered Azamat, pale as death. "But when?"

' "The first time Kazbich comes here – he promised to bring us ten sheep – the rest is my affair. Look out now, Azamat!"

'And that's the way they arranged the thing… if truth be told, not a good thing! I even said so to Pechorin later on, but he only answered me that a wild Circassian girl ought to be happy having such a nice husband as him, because according to their ways he was after all her husband, and that Kazbich was a scoundrel who needed to be punished. Judge for yourself, what answer could I give to counter that?… But at that time I knew nothing about their plot. So one day Kazbich arrived and asks whether we needed some sheep and honey: I told him to bring them the next day. "Azamat!" said Grigory Alexandrovich: "Karagyoz'll be in my hands tomorrow; if Bela isn't here tonight, you'll never see the mount…"

' "Very well!" said Azamat, and galloped off to the village. In the evening Grigory Alexandrovich armed himself and rode out of the fort. How they arranged the thing, I don't know – only in the night they both came back, and the sentry saw that across Azamat's saddle lay a woman whose arms and legs were tied and whose head was wrapped up in a yashmak.'

'And the horse?' I enquired of the staff captain.

'Just a minute, just a minute. Early the next morning Kazbich came and brought ten sheep to sell. Tethering his horse by the fence, he came in to see me; I gave him some tea, because although a scoundrel, he was still my *kunak**.

'We started chatting about this and that… Suddenly I look, Kazbich has shuddered, changed countenance – and he's gone to the window; but the window, unfortunately, looked out onto the backyard. "What's the matter with you?" I asked.

' "My horse!… horse!" he said, trembling all over.

'I could, indeed, hear the clatter of hooves. "It's probably some Cossack that's arrived…"

' "No! *Urus yaman, yaman!*"[10] he roared, and rushed out headlong like a wild cat. In two bounds he was already in the yard; by the gates of the fort the sentry barred his way with his gun; he leapt over the gun and tore off down the road… Dust was swirling in the distance – Azamat was galloping on fiery Karagyoz; Kazbich drew his gun from its case on the run and fired. He stayed still for about a minute until he was convinced he'd missed; then he began to scream, hit his gun against a rock, smashed it to smithereens, threw himself onto the ground and burst out sobbing like a child… People from the fort went and gathered around him – he didn't notice anyone; they stood and talked for a while, then went back. I ordered the money for the sheep to be put down next to him – he didn't touch it, lay there face down like a dead man. Would you believe, he lay like that late into the night, the whole night through?… Only the next morning did he come to the fort and start asking to be told the kidnapper's name. The sentry who saw Azamat untie the mount and gallop away on him didn't think it necessary to conceal it. At this name Kazbich's eyes began to sparkle, and he set out for the village where Azamat's father lived.'

'And the father?'

'Well that's the thing, Kazbich didn't find him: he'd gone away somewhere for about six days, otherwise would Azamat have managed to abduct his sister?

'And when the father returned, neither daughter nor son was there. Such a sly one! I mean, he'd grasped that he'd pay for it if he got caught. And he's been gone ever since: probably joined up with some gang of mountain bandits and laid down his madcap life the other side of the Terek or the Kuban: good riddance!…

* *Kunak* means 'close acquaintance'.

'I confess, quite a bit fell to my lot too. As soon as I found out that Grigory Alexandrovich had the Circassian girl, I put on my epaulettes and sword and went to see him.

'He was lying on the bed in the first room with one hand resting behind his head, and in the other he was holding a pipe that had gone out; the door into the second room was locked and there was no key in the lock. I noticed all this immediately… I started coughing and tapping my heels on the threshold – but he was pretending he couldn't hear.

' "Mr Ensign!" I said, as sternly as possible. "Can't you see that I'm paying you a call?"

' "Ah, hello, Maxim Maximych! Do you want a pipe?" he replied, without raising himself.

' "Excuse me! I'm not Maxim Maximych: I'm Staff Captain."

' "It's all the same. Do you want some tea? If only you knew the worry that's troubling me!"

' "I know everything," I replied, going up to the bed.

' "So much the better: I'm not in the mood for telling you."

' "Mr Ensign, you've committed a misdemeanour for which I too may have to answer…"

' "Come, come! Whatever does it matter? After all, we've been sharing everything equally for a long time now."

' "What are these jokes? Your sword, if you please!"

' "Mitka, my sword!…"

'Mitka brought the sword. Having thus done my duty, I sat down on his bed and said: "Listen, Grigory Alexandrovich, admit that it's not a good thing."

' "What's not a good thing?"

' "Why, the fact that you've abducted Bela… That damned beast Azamat!… Well, admit it," I said to him.

' "And what if I've a fancy for her?…"

'Well, what am I supposed to reply to that?… I was stumped. However, after a bit of silence I told him that if her father started asking for her, she'd have to be given back.

' "Not at all, she won't!"

' "And when he finds out she's here?"

' "But how will he find out?"

'I was stumped again. "Listen, Maxim Maximych!" said Pechorin, raising himself a little: "You're a kind man, after all, and if we give that savage his daughter back, he'll knife her or sell her. The deed's done, there's simply no need to look for ways of making things worse; leave her with me, and you keep my sword…"

' "Show her to me," I said.

' "She's behind that door; I tried to see her myself today without success: she's sitting in the corner, huddled up in her shawl, doesn't speak and doesn't look: timid as a wild chamois. I've hired our innkeeper's wife: she knows Tatar, she's going to look after her and get her accustomed to the idea that she's mine, because she'll belong to no one but me," he added, banging his fist on the table. I agreed to this too… What else was I supposed to do? There are some people you absolutely have to agree with.'

'Well, then?' I enquired of Maxim Maximych: 'Did he really get her accustomed to him, or did homesickness make her wither away in captivity?'

'For pity's sake, why ever homesickness? The same mountains could be seen from the fort as from the village – and these savages need nothing more. And on top of that, Grigory Alexandrovich gave her some sort of present every day: the first few days she proudly pushed them away without a word; the presents were then passed on to the innkeeper's wife and stimulated her eloquence. Ah, presents! What will a woman not do for a bit of coloured cloth!… Well, leaving that aside… For a long time Grigory Alexandrovich struggled with her; he was learning Tatar in the meantime, and she was beginning to understand our language. Little by little she got used to looking at him, at first from under her brows, askance, and she was always grieving, singing her songs in a low voice, so that sometimes I'd start feeling sad as well as I listened to her from the next room. I'll never forget one scene: I was walking past and glanced in at the window. Bela was sitting on the stove-bench with her head drooping on her chest, while Grigory Alexandrovich stood in front of her. "Listen, my peri," he was saying: "you know, don't you, that sooner or later you must be mine – why ever are you just tormenting me? Is it that you love some

Chechen? If that's the case, I'll let you go home now." She gave a barely noticeable shudder and shook her head. "Or," he continued, "am I utterly hateful to you?" She sighed. "Or does your faith forbid you from coming to love me?" She turned pale and was silent. "Believe me, Allah is one and the same for all tribes, and if he permits me to love you, why ever would he forbid you feeling the same for me?" She stared him in the face as if struck by this new idea; in her eyes were expressed mistrust and the desire to be convinced. What eyes! They simply gleamed like two coals.

' "Listen, dear, kind Bela!" continued Pechorin: "you see how I love you; I'm ready to give anything to cheer you up: I want you to be happy, and if you start grieving again, I shall die. Tell me, will you be more cheerful?" She became pensive, keeping her black eyes fixed on him, then smiled affectionately and nodded her head as a sign of agreement. He took her hand and began trying to persuade her to kiss him; she defended herself weakly and only repeated, "Please, please, don't, don't." He began to insist; she started trembling, crying. "I am your captive," she said, "your slave; of course you can force me," and again tears.

'Grigory Alexandrovich struck himself on the forehead with his fist and leapt out into the other room. I went in to see him; he'd given up the struggle and was walking sullenly back and forth. "Well, old chap?" I said to him. "A devil, not a woman!" he replied. "Only I give you my word of honour, she'll be mine…" I shook my head. "Do you want to bet?" he said: "In a week!" – "If you wish!" We shook hands on it and parted.

'The next day he immediately sent a courier to Kizlyar to buy various things, and such a lot of various Persian cloths were brought, you couldn't count them all.

' "What do you think, Maxim Maximych!" he said to me, showing me the presents. "Will an Asiatic beauty withstand such a battery?" – "You don't know Circassian girls," I replied: "they're not at all like Georgian or Transcaucasian Tatar women – not at all. They have their own rules; they're brought up differently." Grigory Alexandrovich smiled and started whistling a march.

'But you know, I turned out to be right: the presents only half worked; she became more affectionate, more trusting – and that was all; so he decided on the final course. One morning he ordered a horse to be saddled, dressed up like a Circassian, armed himself and went in to see her. "Bela!" he said, "you know how much I love you. I resolved to carry you off, thinking that when you got to know me you would come to love me. I was wrong: farewell! Remain here as the absolute mistress of all I have; if you want, return to your father – you're free. I'm at fault before you and must punish myself. Farewell, I'm going – where? How should I know? Perhaps I won't be chasing after a bullet or a sabre-blow for long: remember me then and forgive me." He turned away and reached his hand out to her in farewell. She didn't take his hand, she was silent. Only standing on the other side of the door, I could make out her face through the crack: and I began to feel sorry for her – such a deathly pallor covered that sweet little face! Hearing no reply, Pechorin took several steps towards the door; he was trembling – and shall I tell you? I think he was in a state actually to carry out what he'd been talking about as a joke. That's the kind of man he was, God knows! Only no sooner had he touched the door than she leapt up, broke into sobs and threw her arms around his neck. Would you believe it? Standing on the other side of the door, I started crying too, that is to say, you know, didn't exactly start crying, but, well – silliness!…'

The staff captain fell silent.

'Yes, I admit it,' he said then, pulling at his whiskers. 'I began to feel annoyed that not a single woman had ever loved me like that.'

'And was their happiness long-lived?' I asked.

'Yes, she admitted to us that from the day she'd set eyes on Pechorin, she'd often dreamt about him, and no man had ever made such an impression on her. Yes, they were happy!'

'How boring!' I exclaimed involuntarily. Indeed, I had been expecting a tragic denouement, and to disappoint my hopes so unexpectedly, all of a sudden! 'But surely,' I continued, 'the father guessed she was with you in the fort?'

'Well, yes, he does seem to have suspected. A few days later we learnt the old man had been killed. This is how it happened…'

Again my attention was aroused.

'I ought to tell you that Kazbich imagined Azamat had stolen his horse with his father's consent, at least that's what I suppose. So one time he was lying in wait by the road, about three kilometres outside the village; the old man was returning from a vain search for his daughter; his retinue had fallen behind – it was at dusk – he was riding along pensively at a slow pace, when suddenly Kazbich dived out like a cat from behind a bush, jumped up behind him on the horse, with a blow of his dagger struck him down onto the ground, seized the reins – and was gone; some of the retinue saw it all from a knoll; they tore off to try and catch him, only they couldn't.'

'He recompensed himself for the loss of his mount and took revenge,' I said, in order to elicit my companion's opinion.

'Of course, to their way of thinking,' said the staff captain, 'he was absolutely right.'

I was involuntarily struck by the capacity of the Russian to adapt himself to the customs of those peoples amongst whom he happens to live; I do not know if this mental attribute is worthy of blame or praise, only it proves his unbelievable flexibility and the presence of that clear common sense which forgives evil anywhere that it sees its necessity or the impossibility of its elimination.

Meanwhile the tea had been finished; the horses, which had long been harnessed up, were frozen through in the snow; the moon was pale in the west and already set to sink into its black clouds, which hung on the distant summits like the shreds of a ripped curtain. We left the hut. Contrary to my travelling companion's forecast, the weather had cleared and promised us a quiet morning; chains of dancing stars interlaced in wonderful patterns above the distant horizon and were extinguished one after another as the pallid glow of the east spread across the deep purple vault, gradually illuminating the steep slopes of the mountains, covered in virgin snows. To right and left was the blackness of gloomy, mysterious abysses, and mists, writhing and twisting like snakes, crept into them down the wrinkles of the neighbouring cliffs, as though sensing and fearing the approach of day.

All was quiet in heaven and on earth, as in the heart of a man during morning prayer; only occasionally would a cool wind blow up from the east, slightly lifting the hoar-frost-covered manes of the horses. We got under way; with difficulty did five skinny nags drag our vehicles along the winding road up Mount Gud; we went on foot behind, putting rocks under the wheels when the horses' strength ran out; the road seemed to lead to the sky, because as far as the eye could see it kept on rising, and finally disappeared in a cloud which ever since evening had been resting on the summit of Mount Gud like a kite awaiting its prey; the snow crunched under our feet; the air was becoming so thin that it was painful to breathe; there were continual rushes of blood to the head, but for all that a gratifying sort of feeling spread throughout my veins, and I felt somehow cheerful to be so high above the world: a childish feeling, I cannot argue, but, distancing ourselves from the conventions of society and moving closer to nature, we involuntarily become children: all that has been picked up drops away from the soul, and it is made anew the way it once was and probably will be again some day. Anyone who has happened, like me, to wander over desolate mountains and scrutinise for a long, long time their fantastical forms, swallowing greedily the life-giving air that is spilt in their gorges, will, of course, understand my desire to communicate, to relate, to draw these magical pictures. So finally we finished the climb up Mount Gud, stopped and glanced back: upon it hung a grey cloud, and its cold breath threatened an imminent storm; but in the east all was so clear and golden that we – that is to say, the staff captain and I – completely forgot about the cloud… Yes, the staff captain too: in simple hearts the sense of the beauty and grandeur of nature is a hundred times stronger and keener than in us – enraptured narrators in words and on paper.

'I imagine you've grown accustomed to these magnificent views?' I said to him.

'Yes, sir, you can grow accustomed to the whistling of bullets too – grow accustomed, that is, to concealing the involuntary beating of your heart.'

'I've heard that, on the contrary, some old warriors even find that music pleasant.'

'Well of course, it's a pleasant thing, if you like; only it's still because your heart beats harder. Look,' he added, pointing to the east: 'what a land!'

And to be sure, it is unlikely that I shall be fortunate enough to see such a panorama anywhere else: below us lay the Koyshaur Valley, traversed by the Aragva and another little river as by two silver threads; a bluish mist was slipping down it, fleeing into the neighbouring ravines from the warm rays of morning; to right and left the crests of mountains, each higher than the next, intersected and stretched away, covered with snows and bushes; in the distance – yet more mountains, but not so much as two cliffs resembling one another – and all these snows burned with a roseate lustre so cheerfully, so brightly, it seemed you could just stay and live here for ever; the sun had only just appeared from behind a dark blue mountain, which the accustomed eye alone could have distinguished from a storm cloud; but above the sun was a bloody streak to which my comrade paid particular attention. 'I told you,' he exclaimed, 'there'd be some weather today; we must hurry, or else it may catch us on the Krestovaya. Get going!' he called to the coachmen.

Chains instead of brakes were put under the wheels so that they would not slip, the horses were taken by the bridle and we began to descend; to the right was the crag, to the left such an abyss that a whole little village of Ossetians living at the bottom of it seemed like a swallow's nest; I shuddered, thinking that here along this road where two vehicles cannot pass, some courier or other rides a dozen times a year, often at the dead of night, without climbing out of his jolting carriage. One of our drivers was a Russian peasant from Yaroslavl, the other an Ossetian: the Ossetian led the shaft-horse by the bridle with all possible precautions, having first unharnessed the leading pair – but our carefree Russian lad did not even climb down from the coachman's seat! When I remarked to him that he might have shown a little concern, if only for the sake of my valise, as I had no desire at all to clamber after it into that chasm, he replied to me: 'Hey, master! God willing, we'll get through as well as them: it's not our first time, you know,' – and he was right: we certainly might not have got through, yet we nevertheless did get through, and if everybody gave it a little more thought, they would be convinced that life is really not worth worrying about so much…

But perhaps you want to know the conclusion of the story of Bela? Firstly, I am writing not a fictional tale, but travel notes: consequently I cannot make the staff captain tell the story sooner than he began telling it in reality. And so wait, or, if you wish, turn on a few pages, only I do not advise you to do so, because the crossing of Mount Krestovaya (or, as the learned Gamba calls it, *le Mont St-Christophe*)[11] is worthy of your curiosity. And so we descended from Mount Gud into the Chertova Valley... There is a romantic name! You can already see the nest of an evil spirit amidst unassailable crags – nothing of the sort: the name Chertova Valley derives from the word '*cherta*' and not '*chert*',[12] for at one time the border of Georgia was here. This valley was piled high with snowdrifts which were quite a vivid reminder of Saratov, Tambov and other *nice* places in our fatherland.

'And there's Krestovaya!' the staff captain said to me when we had driven down into the Chertova Valley, indicating a hill covered in a shroud of snow; on its summit was the black shape of a stone cross, and past it led a barely noticeable road, along which people only ride when the road on the hillside is blocked with snow: our drivers announced that there had not yet been any avalanches and, saving the horses, they took us around the hill. At a turn we met five or so Ossetians; they offered us their services and, catching hold of the wheels, with cries they set about pulling and supporting our post-chaises. And the road certainly is dangerous: above our heads to the right hung piles of snow that seemed ready to break off into the gorge at the first gust of wind; the narrow road was partly covered in snow, which gave way under our feet in some places, and in others was turning to ice from the effect of the sun's rays and the night frosts, so that we ourselves made our way forward with difficulty: the horses kept on falling; to the left yawned a deep fissure where a torrent raced, now hiding beneath an icy crust, now foaming and jumping over black rocks. In two hours we had barely managed to skirt around Mount Krestovaya – two kilometres in two hours! Meanwhile storm clouds had come down, hail and snow had fallen; the wind, ripping into the gorges, roared and whistled like the Robber-Nightingale[13], and soon the stone cross had disappeared in the mist, waves of which, each thicker and denser than the last, were rolling in from the east... Incidentally, there exists about that cross the strange but universally accepted legend that Peter I erected it while passing through the Caucasus; but firstly, Peter was only in Dagestan, and secondly, it is written on the cross in large letters that it was erected by order of Mr Ermolov, in 1824 to be precise. But the legend, in spite of the inscription, has taken such root that you really do not know what to believe, all the more since we are not accustomed to believing inscriptions.

We had to descend about another five kilometres down ice-covered cliffs and soft snow to reach the posting station of Kobi. The horses were exhausted, we were frozen through; the blizzard droned on harder and harder, just like our own northern ones; but its wild melodies were sadder, more doleful. 'You too, an exile,' I thought, 'cry for your wide, expansive steppes! There is space there to unfold cold wings, while here you are stifled and cramped, like an eagle that cries and beats itself against the bars of its iron cage.'

'Things are bad!' said the staff captain: 'Look, nothing to be seen all around, only mist and snow. If we don't watch out, we'll topple off into the chasm or get stuck in some hole, and, a little lower down, I expect the Baidara has got so worked up, you won't be able to cross it! This damned Asia! The people, the streams, they're just the same – you can't rely on them at all!' With cries and curses the drivers beat the horses, which snorted, dug their hooves in and did not want to move off for anything in the world, despite the eloquence of the knouts.

'Your Honour!' said one of the drivers eventually. 'We won't get to Kobi today, you know; won't you have us turn off to the left while we can? Over there on the hillside there's something black – a hut, I reckon: travellers always stop there, sir, in bad weather; they say they'll take us, if you give them a tip,' he added, indicating an Ossetian.

'I know, old chap, without your telling me!' said the staff captain. 'These damned beasts! Glad of the opportunity to get a tip out of you.'

'Admit it, though,' I said, 'without them we'd be in a bad way.'

'Quite so, quite so,' he muttered. 'These damned guides! They sense where they can make a profit, as if you couldn't find the way without them.'

And so we turned off to the left and somehow, after a great deal of trouble, reached the meagre refuge, consisting of two huts, built of flags and cobbles and encircled by a wall of just the same type. The ragged owners received us cordially. I learnt afterwards that the Government pays and feeds them on condition that they take in any travellers caught in a storm. 'All's for the best!' I said, sitting down by the fire: 'Now you can finish telling me your story about Bela; I'm sure that wasn't the end of it.'

'And why ever are you so sure?' the staff captain answered me, with a wink and a sly smile.

'Because it's not in the order of things: what began in an unusual way ought to end similarly too.'

'You've guessed it, you know...'

'I'm very glad.'

'It's all right for you to be glad, but I really do get so sad when I remember. She was a splendid girl, that Bela! I got so used to her in the end, as if she'd been a daughter, and she loved me too. I ought to tell you that I have no family: I've not had news of my father or mother for twelve years now, and I didn't think to get myself a wife earlier on – and now, you know, it's unbecoming; I was even pleased I'd found someone to spoil. Sometimes she'd sing us a song or dance the *lezginka*[14]... And how she danced! I've seen our young ladies in the provincial cities, and once, sir, I was even in Moscow in the Nobles' Assembly, twenty years or so ago – but they couldn't compare! Nothing like!... Grigory Alexandrovich dressed her up like a little doll, took care of her, pampered her, and she grew so pretty with us, it was a wonder; the tan wore off her face and hands, a flush appeared on her cheeks... How cheerful she used to be, and she was always making fun of me, the naughty thing... God forgive her!...'

'And what about when you told her of her father's death?'

'We concealed that from her for a long time, until she'd got used to her situation; but when we told her, she cried a bit for a couple of days, and then forgot about it.

'For around four months everything went as well as it possibly could. Grigory Alexandrovich, I think I've already said, had a passionate love of hunting: there were times he'd get such an urge to go off into the forest after boar or goats – yet now he wouldn't even go outside the ramparts of the fort. But then I look, and he's started getting pensive again, walks around the room with his arms folded behind him; then one day, without telling anyone, he goes out shooting – disappears for the whole morning; once, then again, more and more often... This isn't good, I thought: a black cat must have slipped between them!

'One morning I drop in on them – it's as if I could see it now: Bela was sitting on the bed in a black silk coat, all pale, so sad that I took fright.

' "And where's Pechorin?" I asked.

' "Hunting."

' "Did he leave today?" She was silent, as if she had difficulty saying it.

' "No, yesterday," she said finally, with a heavy sigh.

' "I wonder if something's happened to him?"

' "The whole day yesterday I was thinking, thinking," she replied through tears, "thinking up various misfortunes: first it seemed to me he'd been wounded by a wild boar, then a Chechen had dragged him off into the mountains… But now today I just think he doesn't love me."

' "You really couldn't have thought of anything worse, my dear!" She burst out crying, then proudly raised her head, wiped away the tears and continued:

' "If he doesn't love me, who is stopping him sending me home? I'm not forcing him. And if it continues like this, I'll go myself: I'm not his slave – I'm a prince's daughter!…"

'I started to try and talk her round. "Listen, Bela, I mean, he simply can't keep on sitting here as if tied to your apron strings: he's a young man, he likes chasing after game – he'll be out for a bit, then he'll come back; but if you're going to be mournful, he'll get tired of you quicker than ever."

' "You're right, you're right!" she replied: "I'll be cheerful." And, laughing loudly, she grabbed her tambourine, began singing, dancing and jumping around me; but this didn't last long either, she fell down onto the bed once again and covered her face with her hands.

'What was I to do with her? I'd never had dealings with women, you know: I thought and thought how to comfort her, and came up with nothing; for some time we were both silent… A very unpleasant situation, sir!

'Finally I said to her: "Shall we go for a walk onto the ramparts? The weather's splendid!" This was in September. And it certainly was a wonderful day, bright and not hot; all the mountains could be seen as if on a plate. We went and walked up and down the ramparts of the fort for a while in silence; finally she sat down on the turf and I sat down beside her. Well, it's funny to recall, really: I ran after her like some sort of nursemaid.

'Our fort stood on a high spot, and the view from the ramparts was beautiful: on one side a broad plain, pitted with a number of gullies*, ended in forest, which stretched to the very crest of the mountains; upon it here and there was the smoke of villages and wandering herds of horses; on the other side ran a shallow little river, and adjoining it was the dense scrub that covers the flinty heights linking up with the main chain of the Caucasus. We were sitting on the corner of a bastion, so we could see everything in both directions. So I look, and someone's riding out of the forest on a grey horse, closer and closer, and finally he's stopped on the other side of the river, about two hundred metres away from us, and started spinning his horse like a madman. What an odd thing!... "Look, Bela," I said: "you've got young eyes, who's that trick rider: who is it he's come to amuse?..."

'She took a glance and cried out: "It's Kazbich!..."

' "Ah, he's a scoundrel! Come to mock us or something, has he?" I take a good look, definitely Kazbich: his swarthy mug, ragged, dirty as ever. "That's my father's horse," said Bela, grabbing me by the arm; she was trembling like a leaf, and her eyes were sparkling. "Aha!" I thought: "And the blood of brigands isn't silent in you either, my dear!"

' "Come over here," I said to a sentry. "Look to your gun and help that fine fellow down from his horse for me – you'll get a silver rouble." – "Yes, Your Honour; only he doesn't stand still..." – "Tell him to!" I said with a laugh... – "Hey, mate!" shouted the sentry, waving his hand to him. "Hang on a bit, what are you spinning round like a top for?" Kazbich actually did stop and began listening out: he probably thought we were starting to parley with him – no such luck!... My grenadier took aim... bang!... missed; no sooner had the powder flashed in the pan, Kazbich nudged his horse and it leapt aside. He raised himself a little in the stirrups, shouted something in his own language, threatened us with his whip – and was gone.

' "You should be ashamed of yourself!" I said to the sentry.

* Ravines.

31

' "Your Honour, he's gone away to die!" he replied. "They're such a cussed bunch, you can't kill them straight off."

'A quarter of an hour later Pechorin returned from the hunt; Bela threw her arms around his neck, and not a single complaint, not a single reproach about his long absence... Even I got angry with him. "If you please," I said: "just this minute, you know, Kazbich was here on the other side of the river and we were shooting at him: well, will it be long before you stumble upon him? These mountaineers are a vengeful lot: do you think he can't guess that you helped Azamat in part? And I bet he recognised Bela today. I know she was very much to his liking a year ago – he told me so himself – and if he'd been expecting to gather a decent amount of bride-money, he'd probably have asked for her hand..." At this Pechorin became pensive: "Yes," he replied, "we need to be more careful... Bela, from today you mustn't go onto the ramparts of the fort."

'In the evening I had a long discussion with him: I was vexed that he'd changed towards that poor little girl; apart from the fact that he spent half the day out hunting, his manner had become cold, he was rarely affectionate with her, and she was visibly beginning to dry up, her little face had lengthened, her big eyes grown dull. You'd ask her: "What was that sigh about, Bela? Are you feeling sad?" – "No!" – "Do you want anything?" – "No!" – "Do you miss your family?" – "I have no family." It was sometimes the case that for days on end, apart from "yes" and "no", you'd get nothing out of her.

'And it was about just this that I began talking to him: "Listen, Maxim Maximych," he replied: "I have an unfortunate character: whether it was my upbringing that made me so, or God that created me like this, I do not know, I know only the fact that if I am the cause of others' unhappiness, I am no less unhappy myself. That, it goes without saying, is small consolation to them – but the fact is that it is so. In my early youth, from the moment I left the care of my family, I began to take furious delight in all the pleasures that can be had for money, and, it goes without saying, those pleasures became repugnant to me. Then I entered high society, and soon I was tired of society too; I fell in love with society beauties, and I was loved – but their love only inflamed my imagination and vanity, while my heart remained empty...

I began to read, to study – I grew tired of learning too; I saw that neither fame nor happiness depended on it at all, because the happiest people are ignoramuses, and fame is luck, and to achieve it, you need only be artful. Then I became bored... Soon I was transferred to the Caucasus: this was the happiest time of my life. I hoped that boredom could not live under Chechen bullets – in vain: in a month I had grown so accustomed to their buzzing and the proximity of death that, truly, I paid more attention to the mosquitoes – and I became more bored than ever, because I had lost almost my last hope. When I saw Bela in my home, when for the first time, holding her on my knees, I kissed her black locks, fool that I was, I thought she was an angel, sent to me by compassionate fate... Again I was mistaken: the love of a savage is little better than the love of an aristocratic lady; the ignorance and simple-heartedness of the one are just as tiresome as the coquetry of the other. If you like, I still love her, I am grateful to her for a number of quite sweet moments, I will give up my life for her, but I am bored with her. Whether I am a fool, or a villain, I do not know; but it is a certain fact that I am just as much deserving of pity, perhaps more so than she: the soul within me has been spoiled by society, my imagination is restless, my heart insatiable; nothing is enough for me: I grow accustomed to sadness just as easily as to enjoyment, and my life becomes emptier from day to day; one course is left to me: to travel. As soon as it is possible, I shall set off – but not to Europe, God forbid! I shall go to America, to Arabia, to India – perhaps I shall die somewhere on the road! At least I am certain that this final consolation will not soon be exhausted, with the aid of storms and bad roads." He spoke like this for a long time, and his words were engraved on my memory, because I was hearing such things for the first time from a man of twenty-five, and, God grant, for the last... How extraordinary! Now tell me, please,' continued the staff captain, turning to me, 'you seem to have spent time in the capital and not so long ago: surely the youngsters there aren't all like that?'

I replied that there were a lot of people who talked the same way; that there were probably even some who were telling the truth; that disillusionment, however, like all fashions, after starting in the higher strata of society, had descended to the lower ones, who were wearing it out, and that nowadays, those who really were most bored tried to conceal this misfortune as a vice. The staff captain did not understand these subtleties, shook his head and smiled slyly:

'But still, I expect it was the French that brought in the fashion for being bored?'

'No, the English.'

'Aha, so that's it!...' he replied. 'You know, they always were inveterate drunkards!'

I involuntarily recalled a Muscovite lady who asserted that Byron was nothing more than a drunkard. Still, the staff captain's remark was more pardonable: in order to abstain from wine, he, of course, tried to assure himself that all the misfortunes in the world derived from drunkenness.

Meanwhile he continued his story as follows:

'Kazbich didn't appear again. But I don't know why, I couldn't get the idea out of my head that he'd not come without reason and was dreaming up something bad.

'So one day Pechorin tries to persuade me to go hunting boar with him; I turned him down for a long time: well, what was so wonderful about a boar to me! Nonetheless, he still dragged me off with him. We took five soldiers or so and rode off early in the morning. Until ten o'clock we were darting in and out of the reeds and the forest – no beast. "Hey, shouldn't we go back?" I said: "What's the point of being obstinate? It's quite clear, it's just turned out to be an unlucky day!" But Grigory Alexandrovich, despite the intense heat and tiredness, didn't want to go back without bagging something... He was just that sort of person: whatever he thinks of, he has to have it; he was clearly spoilt as a child by his mummy... At midday we finally tracked down a damned boar: bang! bang!... not a chance: got away into the reeds... it was just one of those days!... And so after a little bit of a rest, we set off for home.

'We rode beside one another in silence with our reins hanging loose and had almost reached the fort; only some bushes hid it from us. Suddenly, a shot... We glanced at each other: we were struck by the self-same suspicion... We galloped hell for leather in the direction of the shot; we look, and on the ramparts the soldiers have gathered

34

into a knot and are pointing out into the open, and there there's a rider flying headlong and holding something white on the saddle. Grigory Alexandrovich gave a screech to match any Chechen; gun out of case – and he was off; I went after him.

Fortunately, because of the unsuccessful hunt, our mounts weren't exhausted: they were bursting from under the saddle, and with every instant we were closer and closer... And finally I recognised Kazbich, but I couldn't make out what it was he was holding in front of him. I drew alongside Pechorin then, and shouted to him: "It's Kazbich!..." He looked at me, nodded his head and struck his mount with the lash.

'So finally we were just a gunshot away from him; perhaps Kazbich's horse was exhausted or not as good as ours, and despite all his efforts it wasn't moving ahead that much. I imagine he remembered his Karagyoz at that moment...

'I look, and Pechorin has taken aim with his gun at the gallop... "Don't shoot!" I shout to him: "Save the charge; we'll catch up with him as it is." These damned youngsters! Forever getting heated at the wrong time... But a shot rang out, and the bullet broke the horse's hind leg; in the heat of the moment it made another ten leaps or so, stumbled and fell to its knees. Kazbich jumped off, and then we saw that in his arms he was holding a woman wrapped up in a yashmak... It was Bela... poor Bela! He shouted something to us in his own language and raised his dagger above her... It was no good delaying: I fired in my turn, taking a chance; the bullet probably hit him in the shoulder, because suddenly he lowered his arm... When the smoke cleared, on the ground lay the wounded horse, and alongside it Bela; while Kazbich, who'd abandoned his gun, was scrambling up a crag over the scrub like a cat; I wanted to pick him off from there – but there was no charge ready! We leapt off our horses and rushed up to Bela. The poor thing, she was lying motionless, and streams of blood were pouring from a wound... What a villain: he could at least have struck her in the heart – well, so be it, at least he'd have finished everything off in one go, whereas in the back... a typical scoundrel's blow! She was unconscious. We tore up the yashmak and bandaged the wound up as tight as we could; Pechorin kissed her cold lips to no avail – nothing could bring her round.

35

'Pechorin mounted his horse; I picked her up off the ground and somehow or other sat her on his saddle; he clasped his arm around her and we began to ride back. After a few minutes of silence Grigory Alexandrovich said to me: "Listen, Maxim Maximych, we won't get her back alive like this." – "That's true," I said, and we set the horses off at full speed. A crowd of people was waiting for us at the gates of the fort; we carefully carried the wounded girl to Pechorin's quarters and sent for the doctor. He may have been drunk, but he came; he examined the wound and announced she couldn't live for more than a day; but he was wrong…'

'She recovered?' I asked the staff captain, seizing him by the arm and involuntarily feeling pleased.

'No,' he replied: 'but the doctor was wrong, in that she lived for two more days.'

'So explain to me, how did Kazbich kidnap her?'

'Like this: in spite of Pechorin's ban, she went out of the fort to the river. It was very hot, you know; she sat down on a rock and lowered her feet into the water. Then Kazbich stole up, made a grab for her, stopped her mouth and dragged her into the bushes, and there he leapt up onto his horse and showed a clean pair of heels! She, meanwhile, had managed to shout out; the sentries took alarm, fired, but missed, and at that point we turned up.'

'And why did Kazbich want to abduct her?'

'For pity's sake! These Circassians are a well-known bunch of thieves: they can't help but pinch anything left lying around: they may not even need something, but it still gets stolen… you just have to let them off for that! And what's more, he'd had a fancy for her for a while.'

'And Bela died?'

'She did: only she suffered for a long time, and we went through some real suffering with her too. At about ten o'clock in the evening she came round; we were sitting by the bed; no sooner had she opened her eyes than she began calling for Pechorin. "I'm here beside you, my *dzhanechka* (that's to say – in our language – darling)," he replied, taking her by the hand. "I'm going to die!" she said. We began comforting her, said the doctor had promised to cure her without fail; she shook her head and turned away towards the wall: she didn't want to die!…

'In the night she became delirious; her head was burning; at times a feverish tremor ran all through her body; she spoke disjointedly about her father, brother: she wanted to go home, to the mountains... Then she talked about Pechorin too, gave him various tender names, or reproached him with having stopped loving his *dzhanechka*...

'He listened to her in silence with his head drooping on his arms; but in all that time I didn't notice a single tear on his lashes: whether he really couldn't cry, or was controlling himself, I don't know; as for me, I've never seen anything more pitiable than that.

'Towards morning the delirium passed; for about an hour she lay motionless, pale, and in such a weak state it was scarcely noticeable she was breathing; then she improved, and she began to talk, but what do you think it was about?... Only a dying person has an idea like that, you know!... She started grieving about the fact that she wasn't a Christian, and that her soul would never meet with Grigory Alexandrovich's soul in the other world, and that another woman would be his sweetheart in paradise. I came up with the idea of baptising her before she died: I suggested it to her; she looked at me in indecision and for a long time couldn't utter a word; finally she replied that she would die in the faith in which she was born. A whole day passed like this. How she changed in that day! Her pale cheeks sank, her eyes grew ever so large – her lips burned. She could feel heat inside her, as though a lump of red-hot iron lay in her chest.

'The second night drew on; our eyes never shut, we didn't stir from her bedside. She suffered dreadfully, groaned, and as soon as the pain began to ease, she tried to assure Grigory Alexandrovich that she was better, tried to persuade him to go and have a sleep, kissed his hand, wouldn't let it out of her own. Just before morning she started to feel the pangs of death, began tossing, dislodged her bandage, and the blood began to flow afresh. When the wound had been bandaged, she quietened down for a minute and started asking Pechorin to kiss her. He knelt beside the bed, raised her head a little from the pillow and pressed his lips to hers, which were turning cold; she wound her trembling arms tightly around his neck, as though she wanted to pass her soul on to him in that kiss... No, she did the right thing in dying! Well, what would have become of her if

Grigory Alexandrovich had abandoned her? And that would have happened, sooner or later…

'For half the next day she was quiet, silent and obedient, no matter how our doctor tormented her with poultices and medicine. "For pity's sake!" I said to him: "I mean, you said yourself she was sure to die, so what's the point of all your preparations?" – "It's better, though, Maxim Maximych," he replied, "that my conscience be untroubled." Nice conscience, that!

'After midday she began to be racked by thirst. We opened the windows, but it was hotter outside than in the room: some ice was put by the bed – nothing helped. I knew this unbearable thirst was a sign that the end was near, and I said so to Pechorin. "Water, water!…" she said in a hoarse voice, raising herself up from the bed.

'He turned as white as a sheet, grabbed a glass, poured out some water and handed it to her. I put my hands over my eyes and started saying a prayer, I don't remember which one… Yes, old chap, I've seen a lot – men dying in military hospitals and on the battlefield – but none of that's the same, it's not the same at all!… Plus, to be honest, this is what saddens me: she didn't remember me once before she died; and I think I loved her like a father… Well, may God forgive her!… And to tell the truth: what am I, that anyone should remember me before they die?…

'No sooner had she had a drink of water than she began to feel easier, but about three minutes later she passed away. A mirror was held to her lips – it stayed clear!… I led Pechorin out of the room and we went onto the ramparts of the fort; for a long time we walked up and down alongside one another, not saying a word, our hands folded behind our backs; his face expressed nothing in particular, and I began to feel vexed: in his place I'd have died of grief. Finally he sat down on the ground in the shade and began drawing something in the sand with a stick. Mainly for the sake of decency, you know, I wanted to comfort him, began to talk; he raised his head and burst out laughing… That laughter made my flesh creep… I went to order the coffin.

'To be honest, I busied myself with this partly as a distraction. I had a piece of silk, I lined the coffin with that and decorated it with the Circassian silver galloons that Grigory Alexandrovich had in fact bought for Bela herself.

'The next day, early in the morning, we buried her outside the fort, by the river, alongside the spot where she'd sat for the last time; white acacia and elder bushes have grown up thickly now around her little grave. I almost wanted to put up a cross, but, you know, it's awkward: after all, she wasn't a Christian…'

'And Pechorin?' I asked.

'Pechorin was unwell for a long time, wasted away, poor thing; but from then on we never spoke of Bela: I could see it would be unpleasant for him, so why do it, then? About three months later he was posted to a regiment of Ch***, and he left for Georgia. We haven't met since… Yes, I seem to remember someone told me recently he'd returned to Russia, but it wasn't in corps orders. Still, news is always late reaching the likes of us.'

At this point he launched into a lengthy diatribe on how unpleasant it is to find news out a year late – probably so as to suppress sad memories.

I did not interrupt him and did not listen.

An hour later the opportunity arose to travel on; the blizzard had eased, the sky had cleared, and we set off. Along the way I involuntarily struck up a conversation again about Bela and about Pechorin.

'And have you heard what happened to Kazbich?' I asked.

'To Kazbich? Ah, I don't really know… I've heard that with the Shapsugs on the right flank there's some daredevil Kazbich who rides about at walking pace under our fire, wearing a red coat and bowing most politely whenever a bullet buzzes close by; but it's unlikely to be the same one!…'[15]

At Kobi Maxim Maximych and I parted; I drove off by post-chaise, but he, because of his heavy luggage, was unable to follow on behind me. We did not expect to meet ever again, and yet we did meet, and, if you like, I shall tell you how: it's a tale in itself… Won't you acknowledge, however, that Maxim Maximych is a man worthy of respect?… If you do acknowledge it, then I shall be fully rewarded for my possibly overlong story.

II

Maxim Maximych

After parting with Maxim Maximych, I galloped briskly through the Terek and Daryal gorges, had lunch in Kazbek, took tea in Lars, and had managed to reach Vladikavkaz by supper. I spare you from a description of the mountains, from exclamations which express nothing, from pictures which depict nothing, especially for those who have not been there, and from statistical observations which absolutely no one will bother reading.

I put up in the hotel where all travellers put up, and where at the same time there is nobody to order to roast a pheasant and cook some cabbage soup since the three invalid soldiers to whom it is entrusted are so stupid or so drunk that it is impossible to get any sense out of them.

I was informed that I must stay here another three days since the 'opportunity' from Ekaterinograd had not yet arrived and, conse-quently, was unable to set off back again. What a lost opportunity!… But a bad pun is no comfort to a Russian and, by way of a distraction, I took it into my head to write down Maxim Maximych's story about Bela, not imagining that it would be the first link in a long chain of tales: you see how sometimes an incident of little significance has cruel consequences!… But perhaps you do not know what an 'opportunity' is? It is an escort, composed of half a company of infantry and a cannon, with which transport convoys go through Kabarda from Vladikavkaz to Ekaterinograd.

I spent a very dull first day; early in the morning of the next into the courtyard drives a carriage… Ah! Maxim Maximych!… We met like old acquaintances. I offered him my room. He did not stand on ceremony, even slapped me on the shoulder and twisted his mouth in the manner of a smile. What a character!…

Maxim Maximych had a profound knowledge of the culinary arts: he roasted a pheasant amazingly well, basted it appositely with gherkin brine, and I must admit that without him I would have been obliged to remain on dry rations. A bottle of Kakhetian wine helped us to forget about the modest number of courses, of which there was only the one, and, lighting up our pipes, we settled ourselves down – I by the window, he by the lighted stove, because the day was damp and cold. We were silent. Of what were we to talk?... He had already told me everything there was of interest about himself, while I had nothing to tell. I looked out of the window. Behind some trees could be glimpsed a host of squat little houses, scattered along the bank of the ever more widely spreading Terek, and further off was the blue jagged wall of the mountains, and from behind them peeped Kazbek in its white cardinal's hat. I was bidding them farewell in my thoughts: I had started to feel sad about them...

We sat like that for a long time. The sun was concealing itself behind the cold summits and a whitish mist was beginning to spread through the valleys when the ringing of a harness bell and the shouting of carters were heard outside. Several vehicles carrying some dirty Armenians drove into the hotel yard, followed by an empty travelling carriage; its easy movement, comfortable design and dandified appearance had a certain foreign stamp. Behind it walked a man with big whiskers in a dolman jacket who was quite well dressed for a manservant; it was impossible to mistake his calling, seeing the flashy manner in which he shook out the ashes from his pipe and kept on shouting at the coachman. He was clearly the spoilt servant of a lazy master – a sort of Russian Figaro[16]. 'Tell me, my man,' I called to him through the window, 'what's this – has the "opportunity" arrived, or something?' He gave a rather impertinent look, adjusted his tie and turned away; the Armenian walking beside him replied on his behalf with a grin that it certainly was the opportunity that had arrived and it would be setting off back again the next morning. 'Thank God!' said Maxim Maximych, who had come over to the window at that moment. 'What a wonderful carriage!' he added. 'Probably some official or other going to Tiflis for an investigation. Evidently doesn't know our nice little hills! No, you must be joking, old boy: they're not the friendly type, even an English carriage will get a real good shaking!'

'But who could it be? Let's go and find out...' We went into the passage. At the end of the passage the door into a side room was open. The manservant and a carter were lugging valises into it.

'Listen, old fellow,' the staff captain enquired of him: 'whose is that wonderful carriage?... eh?... It's a fine carriage!...' The manservant did not turn around, but muttered something to himself while untying a valise. Maxim Maximych got angry; he tapped the discourteous fellow on the shoulder and said, 'I'm speaking to you, my man...'

'Whose carriage?... My master's...'

'And who's your master?'

'Pechorin...'

'What's that? What's that? Pechorin?... Oh my God!... He didn't serve in the Caucasus, did he?...' exclaimed Maxim Maximych, pulling at my sleeve. Joy was gleaming in his eyes.

'I believe he did – but I've not been with him long.'

'Well, that's it!... that's it!... Grigory Alexandrovich?... That's his name, isn't it?... Your gentleman and I were close acquaintances,' he added, giving the manservant such a friendly slap on the shoulder that he made him stagger...

'Permit me, sir; you're in the way,' said the latter, frowning.

'You're a one, old fellow!... Don't you know it? Your gentleman and I were inseparable friends, we lived together... But where has the man himself stopped?...'

The servant announced that Pechorin had stopped to dine and spend the night with Colonel N***.

'But won't he be dropping in here this evening?' said Maxim Maximych. 'Or won't you be going to see him about anything, my man?... If you do, then say Maxim Maximych is here; say just that... he knows... I'll give you an eighty-kopek tip...'

The manservant pulled a contemptuous face on hearing such a modest promise, yet assured Maxim Maximych that he would carry out his commission.

'He'll come running straight away, you know!...' Maxim Maximych said to me with a triumphant air: 'I'll go and wait outside the gates for him... Ah, it's a pity I don't know N***.'

Maxim Maximych sat down on the bench outside the gates, and I went off to my room. I confess, I too awaited the appearance of this Pechorin with a certain impatience; although from the staff captain's story I had formed for myself a not very advantageous impression of him, still several features of his character seemed to me remarkable. An hour later, one of the invalids brought a boiling samovar and a teapot. 'Maxim Maximych, do you want some tea?' I called to him out of the window.

'Thank you; I don't feel like it somehow.'

'Hey, have a drink! Look, it's already late, after all, and cold.'

'It's all right; thank you.'

'Well, as you wish!' I started drinking the tea by myself; after about ten minutes in comes my old man: 'You're right, after all: better drink some tea – but I was still waiting… His man went off to see him a long time ago, but something's evidently held him up.'

He hurriedly drank down a cupful, refused a second one and went off out of the gates again in some disquiet: it was clear that the old man was distressed by Pechorin's offhandedness, and all the more since he had recently been telling me of his friendship with him, and just an hour ago had been certain he would come running as soon as he heard his name.

It was already late and dark when I opened the window once more and started calling Maxim Maximych, saying it was time for bed; he mumbled something through gritted teeth; I repeated the invitation – he made no reply.

I lay down on the couch, wrapped up in my greatcoat, having left a candle on the stove-bench; I soon dozed off and would have had a restful sleep if, by then at a very late hour, Maxim Maximych had not woken me when coming into the room. He threw his pipe onto the table, began pacing around the room and poking about in the stove, finally lay down, but spent a long time coughing, spitting and turning from side to side…

'Is it bedbugs biting you?' I asked.

'Yes, bedbugs…' he replied, with a heavy sigh.

The next morning I woke up early; but Maxim Maximych had forestalled me. I found him sitting on the bench by the gates. 'I need to go and see the commandant,' he said, 'so please, if Pechorin comes, send for me…'

I promised. He ran off as though his limbs had been given their youthful strength and flexibility anew.

The morning was fresh, but fine. Golden clouds towered up on the mountains like a new range of aerial mountains; in front of the gates stretched a broad square; beyond it a market was seething with people because it was a Sunday: barefooted Ossetian boys carrying knapsacks filled with honeycomb over their shoulders circled around me; I drove them off: I hadn't any time for them, I was starting to share the disquiet of the good staff captain.

Not ten minutes had gone by before the man we had been awaiting appeared at the end of the square. He was walking with Colonel N*** who, after bringing him as far as the hotel, took his leave of him and turned back for the fort. I sent one of the invalids to fetch Maxim Maximych straight away.

Pechorin's manservant went out to meet him and reported that the harnessing would now begin; he handed him a box of cigars and, after receiving several orders, set off to see to things. His master, having lit a cigar, yawned a couple of times and sat down on the bench on the other side of the gates. I must now draw his portrait for you.

He was of average height; his well-proportioned, slim figure and broad shoulders demonstrated a strong build, capable of bearing all the difficulties of a nomadic life and changing climes, and overcome neither by the dissipation of the life of the capital nor by storms of the spirit; his dusty velvet frock coat, fastened only on the bottom two buttons, allowed one to discern his blindingly clean linen, which pointed to the habits of an orderly man; his soiled gloves seemed made especially to fit his small aristocratic hand, and when he removed one glove, I was amazed by the thinness of his pale fingers. His walk was careless and lazy, but I noticed he did not swing his arms – a sure sign of a certain reticence of character. But then these are my personal remarks, based on my own observations, and I do not wish in the least to force you to believe in them blindly. When he lowered himself onto the bench, his upright figure bent, as though there were not a single bone in his back; the position of his entire body portrayed some sort of nervous weakness; he sat in the way that Balzac's thirty-year-old coquette[17] sits in her downy armchair after an exhausting ball. On a first glance at his face I would not have made him more than twenty-three, although afterwards I was ready to make him thirty. In his smile there was something childlike. His skin had a sort of feminine delicacy; his blond hair, naturally wavy, provided such a picturesque outline for his pale, noble brow, on which only after long observation was it possible to spot traces of the wrinkles that criss-crossed one another and were probably revealed much more clearly in moments of anger or spiritual disquiet. Despite the light colour of his hair, his whiskers and brows were black – a sign of breeding in a man, just as a black mane and a black tail are in a white horse. To finish off the portrait I shall say that he had a slightly snub nose, teeth of blinding whiteness, and brown eyes; of the eyes I ought to say a few words more.

Firstly, they did not laugh when he laughed! Have you happened to notice an oddity of this sort in some people?... It is a sign either of a malicious disposition, or of a profound, constant sadness. From behind partly lowered lashes they shone with a kind of phosphoric brilliance, if one can put it like that. This was not a reflection of spiritual ardour, nor of imagination at play: this was a brilliance similar to the brilliance of smooth steel, blinding, but cold; his gaze – not prolonged, but piercing and uncomfortable, left after it the unpleasant impression of an immodest question, and might have seemed impertinent, had it not been so indifferently calm. All these remarks came to mind perhaps only for the reason that I knew certain details of his life, and perhaps on someone else his appearance would have made a completely different impression; but since you will hear about him from no one but me, you must – like it or not – be content with this depiction. I shall say in conclusion that he was all in all rather good-looking and had one of those original physiognomies that society women particularly like.

The horses were already harnessed; a little bell rang from time to time underneath the shaft bow, and his manservant had already gone over to Pechorin twice to report that all was ready, but Maxim Maximych had still not appeared. Fortunately Pechorin was sunk in a reverie, gazing at the blue teeth of the Caucasus, and seemed not to be hurrying on his way at all. I went up to him. 'If you'd like to wait a little more,' I said, 'you'll have the pleasure of seeing an old acquaintance...'

'Ah, quite so!' he replied quickly: 'I was told yesterday; but wherever is he?' I turned towards the square and saw Maxim Maximych running for all he was worth... A few moments later he was already beside us; he could scarcely breathe; sweat was pouring from his face; wet tufts of grey hair had broken free from beneath his hat and stuck to his forehead; his knees were shaking… he wanted to fling his arms around Pechorin's neck, but the latter quite coldly, albeit with a cordial smile, held out a hand to him. The staff captain was rooted to the ground for a moment, but then greedily grasped his hand with both his own hands; he could not yet speak.

'How pleased I am, dear Maxim Maximych! Well, how are you?' said Pechorin formally.

'And… you?… And you, sir?…' mumbled the old man, with tears in his eyes… 'How long's… it been… and where to now?…'

'I'm going to Persia – and beyond…'

'Surely not right now?… Wait a bit, my dear chap!… Surely we're not to part right now?… We've not seen one another for so long…'

'It's time, Maxim Maximych,' was the reply.

'My God, my God! But where are you hurrying off to like this?… I'd like to tell you so much… ask you so much… Well, then? You've resigned?… How's that?… What've you been doing?…'

'Being bored!' replied Pechorin, smiling.

'And remember our life in the fort?… Splendid hunting country!… You were passionate about shooting, you know… And Bela?…'

Pechorin paled a little and turned away…

'Yes, I remember!' he said, then almost immediately forced a yawn.

Maxim Maximych began begging him to stay with him for another hour or two. 'We'll have a splendid lunch,' he said: 'I've got a brace of pheasants, and the Kakhetian wine here's excellent… it goes without saying, not like it is in Georgia, but of the best quality, though… We'll have a talk… you'll tell me about your life in St Petersburg… Eh?…'

'Truly, I've got nothing to tell, dear Maxim Maximych… However, goodbye, it's time… I'm in a hurry. Thank you for not forgetting me…' he added, taking him by the hand.

The old man furrowed his brow… He was sad and angry, although he tried to conceal it. 'Forgetting!' he grumbled; 'I've not forgotten anything… Well, may God be with you!… I didn't think to meet you like this…'

'Now then, that will do!' said Pechorin, giving him a friendly hug. 'Aren't I really just the same?… What's to be done?… Every man has his own road… Whether we'll be lucky enough to meet again – God knows!…' As he said this, he was already sitting in the carriage, and the coachman had already started to gather up the reins.

'Hang on, hang on!' cried Maxim Maximych suddenly, laying hold of the doors of the carriage: 'I almost completely forgot… Your papers remained with me, Grigory Alexandrovich… I lug them around with me… thought to find you in Georgia, but this is where God let us meet… What am I to do with them?'

'Whatever you like!' replied Pechorin. 'Goodbye!…'

'So you're off to Persia?… And when will you return?…' Maxim Maximych called after him…

The carriage was already far off; but Pechorin gave a sign with his hand which could have been interpreted in the following way: that's unlikely! And to what end?…

For a long time now neither the ringing of the little bell, nor the rumble of the wheels over the flinty road had been audible – but the poor old man stood on the same spot in a deep reverie.

'Yes,' he said finally, trying to adopt an air of indifference, although at times a tear of vexation glittered on his eyelashes, 'of course, we were close acquaintances – but what are close acquaintances in this day and age?… What could he see in me? I'm not rich, not high ranking, and no match at all for him in years either… See what a dandy he's become, how he's been in St Petersburg again… What a carriage!… How much luggage!… And such an aloof manservant!…' These words were pronounced with an ironic smile. 'Tell me,' he continued, turning to me, 'well, what do you think of it?… Well, what demon is it carrying him to Persia now?… Ridiculous, I swear to God, ridiculous!… I mean, I always knew he was a flighty one you couldn't rely on… But it's a pity, really, that he'll come to a bad end… but it can't be otherwise!… And I've always said there's no good in anyone who forgets old friends!…' At this point he turned away to conceal his agitation and went off to walk about the yard by his vehicle, pretending he was examining the wheels, while his eyes were continually filling with tears.

'Maxim Maximych,' I said, going up to him, 'and what sort of papers were they that Pechorin left you?'

'God knows! Notes of some sort…'

'What will you do with them?'

'What? I'll have cartridges made.'

'Better give them to me.'

He looked at me in surprise, muttered something through his teeth, and began rummaging in a valise; and then he pulled out a notebook and threw it scornfully onto the ground; then a second, a third and a tenth met the same fate: there was something childish in his vexation; I began to feel amusement and pity…

'There they all are,' he said; 'congratulations on your find…'

'And can I do anything I like with them?'

'Print them in the newspapers, if you want. What's it to me?… What, am I some friend of his, or a relative?… True, we lived for a long time under the same roof… But then haven't I lived with lots of people?…'

I seized the papers and took them away quickly, fearing the staff captain might repent. Someone soon came to inform us that the 'opportunity' would move off in an hour: I ordered the carriage to be harnessed. The staff captain came into the room when I was already putting on my hat; he did not seem to be preparing for departure: he had a sort of forced, cold air.

'Aren't you coming then, Maxim Maximych?'

'No, sir.'

'And why's that?'

'Well, I've not seen the commandant yet, and I've got to hand over certain official things…'

'But you've been to his house, haven't you?'

'Of course I have…' he said stumblingly, 'but he wasn't in… and I didn't wait.'

I understood him: the poor old man, for the first time in his life perhaps, had abandoned the affairs of service for *personal business*, to use the language of official documents – and how he had been rewarded!

'It's a great shame,' I said to him, 'a great shame, Maxim Maximych, that we have to part ahead of time.'

'How are we uneducated old men supposed to try and keep up with you!... You're young society types, aloof: while you're still here facing Circassian bullets you're just about all right... but if you meet us later on, then you're ashamed even to hold your hand out to the likes of us.'

'I've done nothing to deserve these reproaches, Maxim Maximych.'

'Well, you know, it's just a passing comment; but anyway, I wish you every good fortune and a pleasant journey.'

We said goodbye quite drily. Kind Maxim Maximych had become a stubborn, cantankerous staff captain. And why? Because Pechorin, in absent-mindedness, or for some other reason, had held out his hand to him when he had wanted to fling his arms around Pechorin's neck! It is sad to see a young man lose his best hopes and dreams when the rosy veil through which he has looked at human deeds and feelings is jerked aside in front of him, though there is some hope that he will replace his old delusions with new ones, no less transient, yet at the same time no less sweet... But what do you replace them with at Maxim Maximych's age? Like it or not, the heart will harden and the soul will close up...

I left on my own.

PECHORIN'S JOURNAL

FOREWORD

I recently learnt that Pechorin had died while returning from Persia. This news made me very glad: it gave me the right to print these notes, and I have taken the chance to set my name over somebody else's work. God grant that readers do not punish me for such an innocent forgery!

I must now give some explanation of the reasons that prompted me to submit to the public the heartfelt secrets of a man I never knew. There would be some excuse had I been his friend: the perfidious immodesty of the true friend is comprehensible to all; but I saw him only once in my life on the highway, and consequently cannot have for him that indescribable hatred which, lurking under the cover of friendship, awaits only the death or misfortune of the object of affection to break out over his head in a hail of reproach, advice, mockery and regret.

Reading through these notes, I have become convinced of the sincerity of a man who set his own weaknesses and vices out on display so mercilessly. The history of a human soul, even the pettiest soul, is almost more curious and beneficial than the history of an entire people, especially when it is the result of a mature mind's observations of itself, and when it is written without a vainglorious desire to arouse sympathy or surprise. Rousseau's Confessions[18] have the immediate shortcoming that he read them to his friends.

And so the desire for benefit alone made me print fragments from a journal that came to me by chance. Although I have changed all the proper names, those who are spoken of in it will probably recognise themselves, and perhaps they will find some justification for the actions for which up until now they have blamed a man who henceforth no longer has anything in common with this world: we almost always excuse what we understand.

I have put in this book only what relates to Pechorin's stay in the Caucasus; in my possession there still remains a thick notebook where he tells his whole life story. Someday it too will present itself for society's judgement; but I do not now dare to take this responsibility upon myself for many important reasons.

Perhaps some readers will wish to learn my opinion of Pechorin's character? My reply is the title of this book. 'But that's a wicked irony!' they will say. I do not know.

1

Taman

Taman is the nastiest little hole of all Russia's coastal towns. I very nearly died of hunger there, and on top of that somebody tried to drown me. I arrived by post-chaise late at night. The coachman stopped his tired team of horses by the gates of the only stone building at the entrance to the town. When he heard the ringing of the bell, a Black Sea Cossack sentry, still half-asleep, cried out in a wild voice: 'Who goes there?' A sergeant and a constable emerged. I explained to them that I was an officer travelling on official business to a detachment in the field, and began demanding official quarters. The constable led us around the town. No matter what hut we came to, it was occupied. It was cold, I hadn't slept for three nights, I was worn out and beginning to get angry. 'Take me anywhere, you scoundrel! To the devil, if you like, but take me somewhere!' I shouted. 'There is one more billet,' replied the constable, scratching his head: 'but Your Honour won't like it; it's unclean!' Without understanding the precise meaning of the final word, I ordered him to go ahead, and after a long time wandering down muddy alleyways where I could see only ramshackle fences on either side, we rode up to a small hut right on the seashore.

The full moon shone on the rush roof and white walls of my new lodgings; in the yard, which was surrounded by a stone enclosure, there stood a second, crooked shack, smaller and more ancient than the first. The shore descended precipitously to the sea almost at its very walls, and down below, with an uninterrupted murmuring, there splashed the dark blue waves. The moon looked quietly upon the restless, but submissive element, and in its light I could distinguish, far from the shore, two ships, whose black rigging stood in motionless silhouette on the pale line of the horizon like a spider's web. 'There are boats in the harbour,' I thought: 'tomorrow I'll be leaving for Gelendzhik.'

I had a Cossack from the Line with me who carried out the duties of a batman. Ordering him to unload my valise and let the driver go, I started calling for the master – silence; I knocked – silence… what's this? Finally a boy of about fourteen crawled out of the doorway.

'Where's the master?' – '*Ne-ma*.'[19] – 'What do you mean: not at all?' – 'Not at all.' – 'And the mistress?' – 'She's away at the village.' – 'Who'll open the door for me, then?' I said, kicking it. The door opened by itself; a wave of damp came out of the hut. I lit a sulphur match and lifted it up to the boy's nose: it illuminated two white eyes. He was blind, totally blind from birth. He stood motionless before me, and I began examining the features of his face.

I confess I have a strong prejudice against all who are blind, one-eyed, deaf, dumb, legless, armless, hunchbacked and so on. I've noticed that there's always some strange relationship between a man's appearance and his soul: it's as if with the loss of a limb the soul loses one feeling or another.

And so I began examining the blind boy's face; but what can you read in a face that has no eyes?… I'd been gazing at him for a long time with involuntary pity when suddenly a scarcely perceptible smile flickered across his thin lips and, I don't know why, it made the most unpleasant impression on me. In my head was born the suspicion that this blind boy wasn't so blind as it seemed; in vain I tried to assure myself that it's not possible to fake wall eyes, and anyway, to what end? But what can you do? I'm often inclined to prejudices…

'Are you the mistress' son?' I finally asked him. – '*Ni*.'[20] – 'Who are you, then?' – 'A poor orphan.' – 'And does the mistress have any children?' – '*Ni*, she used to have a daughter, but she ran away across the sea with a Tatar.' – 'What Tatar's that?' – 'The devil knows! A Crimean Tatar, a boatman from Kerch.'

I went into the hut: two benches and a table plus a huge chest beside the stove comprised all its furniture. Not a single icon on the wall – a bad sign! The sea breeze burst in through a broken pane of glass. I pulled the stub of a wax candle out of my valise and, after lighting it, began setting out my things, standing my sabre and rifle in the corner, putting my pistols on the table, and spreading my cloak out on a bench; my Cossack spread his out on the other one, and ten minutes later he started snoring, but I couldn't get to sleep: I kept on seeing the boy with the white eyes before me in the gloom.

About an hour passed like this. The moon shone into the window and its beam played across the earthen floor of the hut. Suddenly a shadow flitted by on the bright strip that cut across the floor. I half rose and glanced out of the window: somebody ran past it a second time and disappeared God knows where. I couldn't imagine that this being had run down the slope of the shore; however, there was nowhere for it to have gone otherwise. I got up, threw on my Caucasian quilted jacket, fastened on my belt and dagger and went ever so quietly out of the hut; the blind boy was coming towards me. I hid by the fence, and he walked past me with a sure but cautious step. He was carrying some sort of bundle under his arm and, turning towards the harbour, he started to descend a narrow and steep path. 'On that day the dumb shall give voice and the blind shall see,'[21] I thought, following him at such a distance as not to let him out of sight.

Meanwhile the moon began to be clothed in clouds and a mist rose up out at sea; through it the lantern on the stern of the nearer ship was scarcely twinkling; by the shore there glinted the foam on the rocks that threatened to sink it at any minute. Descending with difficulty, I made my way down a steep slope, and then I saw the blind boy stop for a moment before turning right at the bottom; he was walking so close to the water that it seemed a wave was always about to seize him and carry him off; but this was evidently not his first walk, judging by the confidence with which he stepped from stone to stone and avoided the crevices. Finally he stopped, as though listening out for something, squatted onto the ground and put the bundle down beside him. I observed his movements, hidden behind a rock face jutting out from the shore. After a few minutes a white figure appeared from the opposite direction; it went up to the blind boy and sat down beside him. From time to time the wind carried their conversation to me.

'Well, blind boy?' said a woman's voice: 'the storm's a big one; Yanko won't come.' – 'Yanko's not afraid of a storm,' he replied. 'The mist's thickening,' retorted the woman's voice again, with an expression of sadness.

'It's easier to get past the guard boats in the mist,' came the reply. – 'But what if he drowns?' – 'Well, so what? You'll go to church on Sunday with no new ribbon.'

A silence ensued; one thing, however, had amazed me: the blind boy

55

had spoken to me in a Little Russian dialect, but now he was expressing himself in perfect Russian.

'You see, I'm right,' the blind boy spoke again, clapping his hands: 'Yanko's not afraid either of the sea, or the winds, or the mist, or the coastal guards; listen carefully now: that's not the water splashing, you can't fool me – that's his long oars.'

The woman leapt up and started peering into the distance with an air of anxiety.

'You're delirious, blind boy,' she said, 'I can't see anything.'

I confess, however hard I tried to distinguish anything resembling a boat in the distance, it was without success. Ten minutes or so passed like this; and then between the mountainous waves there appeared a black dot: at times it would grow bigger, at others smaller. Slowly rising onto the crests of the waves and rapidly descending from them, a rowing boat was nearing the shore. Courageous was the boatman who had resolved to set off a distance of twenty kilometres across the strait on a night like this, and important must have been the reason prompting him to do so! With this thought, and with an involuntary beating of my heart, I gazed at the poor boat; but it dived like a duck and then, rapidly flapping its oars, as if they were wings, it leapt out of the abyss amidst a spray of foam; and I thought at any moment it would strike against the shore with a crash and be smashed to smithereens, but it deftly turned sideways on and leapt into a little bay unharmed. Out of it got a man of medium height in a Tatar sheepskin hat; he waved, and all three set about pulling something out of the boat; the load was so great that I still can't understand how it hadn't sunk. Taking a bundle each on their shoulders, they set off along the shore, and I soon lost sight of them. I had to return home; but, I confess, all these strange things alarmed me, and I could hardly wait for the morning.

My Cossack was very surprised when, on waking, he saw me fully dressed; however, I didn't tell him the reason. After some time admiring through the window the blue sky, strewn with ragged little clouds, and the distant shore of the Crimea, which stretches in a lilac band and ends in a crag on whose summit is a white lighthouse tower, I set off for the fort of Fanagoria to find out from the commandant the time of my departure for Gelendzhik.

But alas, the commandant could tell me nothing definite. The boats standing in the harbour were all either guard boats or merchantmen which had not yet even begun to be loaded. 'Perhaps in three or four days the mail boat will come,' said the commandant, 'and then we'll see.' I returned home sullen and angry. I was met in the doorway by my Cossack with a frightened face.

'It's bad, Your Honour!' he said to me.

'That's right, old fellow, God knows when we'll be away from here!' At this point he became even more alarmed and, leaning towards me, he said in a whisper:

'This place is unclean! I met a Black Sea sergeant today; I know him – he was in our detachment last year; when I told him where we'd put up, he says to me: "That place is unclean, old fellow, the people are bad!…" And to be sure, what sort of blind boy's that! Goes everywhere by himself, to the market for bread and to fetch water too… it's quite clear they're used to it here.'

'Well, so what? Has the mistress at least appeared?'

'While you were out today an old woman arrived, and her daughter with her.'

'What daughter? She hasn't got a daughter.'

'Well God knows who she is, if she's not her daughter; there's the old woman now, sitting in her hut.'

I went into the shack. The stove had been heated up good and hot, and a meal quite lavish for poor people was cooking inside it. To all my questions the old woman replied that she was deaf and couldn't hear. What was to be done with her? I turned to the blind boy, who was sitting in front of the stove and adding brushwood to the fire. 'Come on, you little blind devil,' I said, taking hold of his ear: 'talk, where were you headed with the bundle in the night, eh?' Suddenly my blind boy started crying, shouting, groaning: 'Where was I going?… I wasn't going anywhere… With a bundle? What bundle?' This time the old woman heard and began grumbling: 'Goes making things up, and accusing a cripple too! Why are you on at him? What's he done to you?' I was tired of it and I went outside, firmly resolved to find the key to this riddle.

I wrapped myself in my Caucasian felt cloak and sat down on a rock by the fence, gazing into the distance; before me stretched the sea, stirred up by the storm during the night, and its monotonous noise, like the murmuring of a town as it falls asleep, reminded me of the old days, carried my thoughts away to the north, to our cold capital. Stirred by memories, I became lost in a reverie… About an hour passed like this, perhaps even more… Suddenly something resembling a song struck my ear. Yes, it was a song, and a fresh female voice – but where from?… I listened intently – it was a strange tune, now drawn out and sad, now quick and lively. I looked around – there was nobody about; I listened intently once more – it was as if the sounds were falling from the sky. I raised my eyes: on the roof of my hut stood a girl in a striped dress with her braids hanging loose, a real mermaid. Shielding her eyes from the sun's rays with her palm, she was peering fixedly into the distance, now laughing and talking to herself, now breaking into song once more.

I memorised that song word for word:

Following their freedom free,
Now across the green sea
All the little ships do go,
Little ships with white sails.
And amongst those little ships
There's my rowing boat,
A rowing boat quite unrigged,
A boat with two oars.
Should by chance a storm break out,
Then all the little old ships
Will raise wings aloft to be
Swept away across the sea.
I shall bow down to the sea
Low as low can be:
'Don't you touch, you angry sea,
My wee rowing boat:
My wee rowing boat it bears
A cargo that is precious,
Steering it through the dark night
Is a wild, madcap fellow.'

It involuntarily occurred to me that I had heard the same voice in the night; I fell into thought for a moment, and when I looked at the roof once more, the girl wasn't there. Suddenly she ran past me, singing something else, and, clicking her fingers, ran in to the old woman, and at this point an argument broke out between them. The old woman got angry, while she roared with laughter. And then I saw my undine skipping along again; upon drawing level with me, she stopped and stared fixedly into my eyes as though surprised at my presence; then she turned nonchalantly and went off quietly towards the harbour. That wasn't the end of it: she was hanging around my quarters all day: the singing and the jumping didn't cease for a moment. A strange creature! There were no signs of madness in her face; on the contrary, her eyes came to rest on me with lively perspicacity, and those eyes seemed to be endowed with some magnetic power, and each time it was as if they awaited a question. But no sooner did I begin to speak than she ran off with a sly smile.

I had certainly never seen such a woman. She was far from being a beauty, but I also have my prejudices regarding beauty. There was a lot of breeding in her... breeding in women, as in horses too, is a great thing; this discovery belongs to *la jeune France*[22]. It (that is breeding, and not *la jeune France*) shows for the most part in the walk, the hands and feet; the nose in particular means a lot. A regular nose is rarer in Russia than a small foot. My songstress seemed no older than eighteen. The unusual suppleness of her body, the particular tilt of the head that was hers alone, the long light brown hair, a sort of golden bloom on her lightly tanned skin at the neck and shoulders, and in particular the regular nose – all this I found enchanting. Although in her sidelong glances I read something wild and suspicious, although in her smile there was something indefinite, still such is the power of prejudices: the regular nose drove me out of my mind; I imagined I had found Goethe's Mignon[23], that whimsical creation of his German imagination – and there was, indeed, much similarity between them: the same rapid shifts from extreme restlessness to complete immobility, the same mysterious speeches, the same jumps, strange songs...

Towards evening, stopping her in the doorway, I struck up the following conversation with her:

'Tell me now, my beauty,' I asked: 'what were you doing on the roof today?' – 'Looking to see where the wind was blowing from.' – 'Why do you need to know?' – 'Whence the wind, thence happiness too.' – 'Well then? Summoning up happiness with your song, were you?' – 'Where there's singing there's happiness too.' – 'But what if your singing should bring you misfortune?' – 'Well, so what? Where it isn't better, it'll be worse, and from bad back to good isn't far.' – 'Who taught you that song?' – 'Nobody taught it me; if I take it into my head, then I start to sing; the person meant to hear will hear; and anyone that shouldn't hear won't understand.' – 'And what's your name, my songstress?' – 'The one that christened me knows.' – 'And who was it christened you?' – 'How should I know?' – 'What a secretive one! But then I have found something out about you.' (Her expression didn't change, her lips didn't stir, as though it was nothing to do with her.) 'I've found out that you went down to the seashore last night.' And at this point I very pompously related everything I'd seen to her, thinking to embarrass her; not in the least! She burst out laughing as loud as could be. 'You've seen a lot, but don't know much; and what you do know, keep it under lock and key.' – 'And what if I took it into my head, for example, to inform the commandant?' – and at this point I pulled a very serious, even stern face. She suddenly jumped, broke into song and disappeared, like a little bird started out of the bushes. My final words were quite out of place; I didn't suspect their importance then, but subsequently I had occasion to repent of them.

It had just got dark when I ordered my Cossack to heat up the kettle the way you do in the field, lit a candle and sat down by the table, taking the occasional puff on my travelling pipe. I was already finishing my second glass of tea when suddenly the door creaked and the light rustling of a dress and footsteps were to be heard behind me; I gave a start and turned – it was she, my undine! She sat down opposite me, quietly and wordlessly, and directed her eyes at me, and I don't know why, but that gaze seemed to me wonderfully tender; it reminded me of one of those glances which in the old days had toyed so despotically with my life. She seemed to be awaiting a question, but I was silent, filled with inexplicable confusion. Her face was covered with a dull pallor that revealed spiritual disquiet; her hand wandered aimlessly over the table, and I noticed it trembling slightly; at times her breast was heaving, at times she seemed to be restraining her breathing. I was beginning to get tired of this comedy and I was about to break the silence in the most prosaic way, that is, by offering her a glass of tea, when suddenly she leapt up, wrapped her arms around my neck, and a moist, fiery kiss rang out on my lips. My eyes grew dim, my head span, I squeezed her in my embrace with all the strength of youthful passion, but she slipped like a snake through my arms, whispering in my ear: 'Tonight, when everyone's asleep, come out onto the seashore,' and flew out of the room like an arrow. In the porch she overturned the kettle and a candle standing on the floor. 'What a she-devil!' shouted the Cossack, who had settled down on the straw and was dreaming of warming himself up with the remainder of the tea. Only at this point did I recover myself.

A couple of hours later, when all had fallen quiet on the quayside, I woke my Cossack up: 'If I fire my pistol,' I said to him: 'then run to the seashore.' He opened his eyes wide and replied mechanically: 'Yes, Your Honour.' I stuck a pistol in my belt and went outside. She was waiting for me on the edge of the slope; her clothing was light, to say the least; a little shawl was wrapped around her supple body.

'Follow me!' she said, taking me by the hand, and we began to descend. I've never understood how I didn't break my neck; at the bottom we turned right and went by the same route along which I had followed the blind boy the night before. The moon had not yet risen, and just two little stars, like two salutary beacons, twinkled in the dark blue vault. The heavy waves rolled in rhythmically and evenly one after another, scarcely lifting the solitary rowing boat moored at the seashore. 'Let's get into the boat,' said my companion. I hesitated – I'm not a lover of sentimental trips at sea; but this was no time to retreat. She jumped into the boat, I followed her, and I'd not yet had time to recover myself before I noticed that we'd pushed off. 'What does this mean?' I said angrily. – 'It means,' she replied, sitting me down on a crossbench and wrapping her arms around my body: 'it means I love you...' And her cheek pressed against mine, and I felt her ardent breath on my face. Suddenly something fell noisily into the water: I grabbed at my belt – no pistol. Oh, at this point a terrible suspicion crept into my soul, the blood rushed to my head! I looked around – we were about a hundred metres from the shore, and I can't swim! I tried to push her away from me – she clung onto my clothes like a cat, and suddenly a mighty shove all but threw me into the sea. The boat began rocking, but I righted myself, and a desperate struggle began between us; fury gave me added strength, but I soon noticed I was the inferior of my opponent in dexterity… 'What do you want?' I shouted, squeezing her little hands tightly; her fingers cracked, but she didn't cry out: her snakelike nature withstood the torture.

'You saw,' she replied: 'you'll inform!' – and with a supernatural effort she toppled me over onto the boat's side; we both hung out of the boat from the waist up; her hair was touching the water; the moment was decisive. I wedged my knee against the bottom of the boat, grabbed her with one hand by her braid, with the other by the throat, she let go of my clothes, and I instantly threw her into the waves.

It was already quite dark; a couple of times there were fleeting glimpses of her head amidst the foam of the sea, and I saw nothing more…

On the bottom of the boat I found half an old oar and somehow, after lengthy efforts, I moored at the quayside. Making my way along the shore to my hut, I involuntarily peered towards where the blind boy had been waiting for the nocturnal boatman the night before; the moon was already rolling across the sky, and it seemed to me that someone in white was sitting on the seashore; I stole up, excited by curiosity, and lay down in the grass above the precipice of the shore; by poking my head out a little I had a good view from the crag of everything that was happening down below, and wasn't very surprised, but was almost pleased, when I recognised my mermaid. She was wringing the sea foam out of her long hair; the wet shirt outlined her supple body and high breasts. Soon a rowing boat appeared in the distance, it approached quickly; out of it, as on the night before, stepped a man in a Tatar hat, but he had his hair cut like a Cossack, and a large knife stuck out of his belt. 'Yanko,' she said: 'all's lost!' Then their conversation continued, but so quietly that I couldn't make anything out. 'And where's the blind boy?' said Yanko finally, raising his voice. 'I've sent him,' was the reply. After a few minutes the blind boy turned up, lugging a sack on his back which was put into the boat.

'Listen, blind boy!' said Yanko: 'you look after that place… you know? There's valuable goods there… Tell' – I couldn't hear the name properly – 'I'm his servant no longer; things have taken a bad turn, he'll see me no more; it's dangerous now; I'll go and look for work somewhere else, and he'll never find another man so bold. And tell him if he'd paid a bit better for his labours, then Yanko wouldn't have abandoned him; but there's a road for me anywhere, wherever the wind blows and the sea roars!' After some silence Yanko continued: 'She'll come with me; she can't stay here; and tell the old woman, say, it's time you died, you've lived long enough, the time's come to be off. She won't be seeing us again.'

'What about me?' said the blind boy, in a plaintive voice.

'What use are you to me?'

Meanwhile my undine leapt into the boat and waved to her comrade; he put something into the blind boy's hand, adding: 'Here, buy yourself some gingerbread.' – 'Is that all?' said the blind boy. – 'Well here's some more then,' – and the coin that dropped rang as it hit against a rock. The blind boy didn't pick it up. Yanko got into the boat; the wind was blowing off the shore: they raised a small sail and quickly sped away. For a long time by the light of the moon the white sail could be glimpsed amidst the dark waves; the blind boy still sat on the seashore, and then I seemed to hear something like sobbing: the blind boy was definitely crying, and for a long, long time… I began to feel sad. And why did fate have to toss me into a peaceful circle of *honest smugglers*? Like a stone thrown into the smooth water of a spring I had disturbed their tranquillity, and like the stone had almost gone to the bottom myself!

I returned home. In the porch the burnt-out candle was crackling in a wooden bowl, and my Cossack, contrary to my order, was fast asleep, holding onto his rifle with both hands. I left him in peace, took the candle and went into the hut. Alas! My casket, my silver-mounted sabre, my dagger from Dagestan – a present from an acquaintance – all had disappeared. It was at this point I guessed what things that damned blind boy had been lugging. Waking the Cossack up with a rather impolite shove, I gave him a telling-off, got angry, but there was nothing that could be done! And wouldn't it be ridiculous to complain to the authorities that a blind boy had robbed me and an eighteen-year-old girl had almost drowned me? Thank God, in the morning the opportunity arose to go, and I left Taman. What happened to the old woman and the poor blind boy – I don't know. And what have human joys and calamities got to do with me, a travelling officer, with a requisition for post-horses on Government business, what's more!...

2

Princess Mary

I arrived in Pyatigorsk yesterday and took an apartment on the edge of town, at the very highest point, at the foot of Mashuk: during storms the clouds will come right down to my roof. At five o'clock this morning, when I opened the window, my room was filled with the scent of the flowers growing in the modest front garden. The branches of flowering cherry trees look into my window, and at times the wind covers my writing desk with their white petals. I have wonderful views on three sides. To the west five-peaked Beshtu shows blue like 'the last of the clouds of the scattering tempest'[24]; to the north rises Mashuk, like a shaggy Persian hat, and covers all that part of the sky; looking east is more fun: before me down below are the bright colours of the nice, new, clean little town, the noise of the medicinal springs, the noise of the multilingual crowd – and there, further on, the mountains pile up like an amphitheatre, ever bluer and mistier, and on the edge of the horizon stretches a silver chain of snowy summits, beginning with Kazbek and ending with the twin-peaked Elbrus… It's fun living in country like this! A gratifying sort of feeling has spread through my every vein. The air's pure and fresh, like a child's kiss; the sun's bright, the sky's blue – what more, one wonders, could you want? What need do you have here of passions, desires, regrets?… However, it's time. I'll go to the Elisavetinsky Spring: it's said that the whole of spa society gathers there in the morning.

After going down into the centre of town, I set off along the boulevard, where I met several sad groups going slowly uphill; for the most part these were the families of steppe landowners: this could be guessed straight away from the worn, old-fashioned frock coats of the husbands, and the refined costumes of the wives and daughters: they evidently had all the *spa* youth accounted for already, because they looked at me with tender curiosity: the St Petersburg cut of my frock coat misled them, but they soon recognised my army epaulettes and turned away in disgust.

The wives of the local officials, the mistresses of the spa, so to speak, were better disposed; they have lorgnettes, they pay less attention to one's uniform, in the Caucasus they're used to meeting an ardent heart beneath a numbered button, and an educated mind beneath a white cap.[25] These ladies are very sweet, and stay sweet for a long time! Every year their admirers are replaced by new ones, and perhaps it's in this that the secret of their untiring kindliness lies. Going up the narrow path to the Elisavetinsky Spring I overtook a crowd of men, both civilian and military, who, as I learnt later on, make up a particular class of people waiting for the 'moving of the waters'[26]. They drink – but not water, don't do much walking, womanise only in passing: they gamble and complain of boredom. They're dandies: lowering their wickered glasses into a sulphate well, they strike academic poses; the civilians wear light blue ties, the soldiers have frills sticking out from under their collars. They profess a deep contempt for provincial houses and sigh for the aristocratic drawing rooms of the capital, to which they're not admitted.

Finally here's the well… On a small square nearby, a little build -ing with a red roof stands over a bath, and a little further off is a gallery where people walk when it rains. A few wounded officers with crutches, pale and sad, were sitting on a bench. A few ladies were walking with rapid steps to and fro across the square, waiting for the effect of the waters. Among them were two or three pretty little faces. Below paths covered in vines that hid the slopes of Mashuk there were occasional glimpses of the colourful bonnets of lovers of solitude in another's company, because alongside such a bonnet I always spotted either an army cap or an ugly round hat. On the steep cliff where a pavilion called the Aeolian Harp stands, lovers of views were hanging about and directing their telescopes at Elbrus; among them were two private tutors with their pupils who've come to treat their scrofula.

I'd stopped, out of breath, on the mountain's edge and, leaning against the corner of the little building, had begun to examine the picturesque surroundings, when suddenly I hear a familiar voice behind me.

'Pechorin! Have you been here long?'

I turn around: Grushnitsky! We embraced. I'd met him in

detachment on active service. He'd got a bullet-wound in the leg and had left for the spa about a week before me.

Grushnitsky's a cadet. He's been serving for only a year and, observing a particular kind of dandyism, wears the heavy greatcoat of a private soldier. He has a soldier's Cross of St George. He has a good figure, is swarthy and black-haired; to look at, you might think he was twenty-five, though he's scarcely twenty-one. He throws his head back when he speaks and is constantly twirling his moustache with his left hand, as the right leans on a crutch. His speech is rapid and mannered: he's one of those people who have grand ready phrases for all life's eventualities, who aren't touched by the simply beautiful, and who drape themselves pompously in extraordinary emotions, elevated passions and exceptional sufferings. To produce an effect – that's their pleasure; romantic provincial girls are mad about them. As old age approaches they become either sedate landowners or drunkards – sometimes both the one and the other. There are often many good qualities in their souls, but not a trace of poetry. Grushnitsky's passion was declamation: he'd bombard you with words the moment the conversation departed from the range of ordinary concepts; I could never argue with him. He doesn't reply to your objections, he doesn't listen to you. As soon as you pause he begins a long tirade, which ostensibly has some sort of connection with what you've said, but which is in fact only the continuation of his own speech.

He's quite sharp: his epigrams are often amusing, but are never well directed and spiteful: he'll not kill anyone with just a single word; he doesn't know people and their weak points, because all his life he's been preoccupied only with himself. His aim is to make himself the hero of a novel. So often has he tried to convince others that he's a being not meant for this world, doomed to some secret sufferings, that he's almost become convinced of it himself. And that's why he wears his soldier's heavy greatcoat so proudly. I've rumbled him, and he doesn't like me for that, although outwardly we enjoy the most friendly relations. Grushnitsky is reputed to be outstandingly brave; I've seen him in action; he brandishes his sabre, shouts and rushes forward with his eyes screwed up. That's not Russian bravery somehow!…

I don't like him either: I sense that someday he and I will run into each other on a narrow road and things will turn out badly for one of us.

His arrival in the Caucasus is also a consequence of his romantic fanaticism: I'm certain that on the eve of departure from his father's estate, with a gloomy air he told some pretty neighbour that he wasn't leaving simply to serve in the army, but that he was seeking death because... at this point he probably put his hand over his eyes and continued thus: 'No, you shouldn't know that! Your pure soul will shudder! And anyway, why? What am I to you? Will you understand me?...' and so on.

He told me himself that the reason that had prompted him to join the K. Regiment would remain an eternal secret between him and the heavens.

And yet whenever he throws off the tragic mantle Grushnitsky is quite nice and amusing. I'm curious to see him with women: it's then, I imagine, that he really tries hard!

We met like old and close acquaintances. I began questioning him about the way of life at the spa and about the noteworthy characters.

'We lead a rather prosaic life,' he said with a sigh: 'those who drink water in the morning are lethargic, like all sick people, while those who drink wine in the evening are intolerable, like all healthy people. There are elements of female society; but there's no great comfort in them: they play whist, dress badly and speak terrible French. From Moscow this year there's only Princess Ligovskaya with her daughter; but I'm not acquainted with them. My soldier's greatcoat is like a stamp of rejection. The sympathy it arouses is as hard to bear as charity.'

At this moment two ladies walked past us towards the well: one middle-aged, the other young and slim. I couldn't make out their faces, hidden by their bonnets, but they were dressed according to the strict rules of the best taste: nothing superfluous. The second one was wearing a high-necked dress *gris de perles*[27]; a light silk scarf was wound about her supple neck. Snug boots *couleur de puce*[28] fitted her slender little foot so nicely at the ankle that even someone uninitiated in the mysteries of beauty would certainly have gasped, if only in surprise. Her light, but noble tread had something virginal about it, something eluding definition, but comprehensible to the eye. When she walked past us there wafted from her that inexpressible fragrance sometimes given off by a note received from a woman you hold dear.

'There's Princess Ligovskaya,' said Grushnitsky, 'and with her is her daughter, Mary, as she calls her in the English manner. She's been here only three days.'

'Yet you already know her name?'

'Yes, I heard it by chance,' he replied, blushing. 'I confess, I've no desire to meet them. These proud aristocrats look upon us army men as savages. And what is it to them if there's a mind beneath a numbered cap and a heart beneath a heavy greatcoat?'

'That poor greatcoat!' I said, with a smirk. 'And who's that gentleman going up to them and handing them glasses so obligingly?'

'Oh, that's a Moscow dandy, Rayevich! He's a gambler: that's clear straight away from the huge gold chain looped across his blue waistcoat. And what's that heavy walking stick – just like Robinson Crusoe's[29]! And the beard's right too, and the hairstyle *à la moujik*[30].'

'You've got it in for the whole human race.'

'And not without reason…'

'Oh, really?'

At this moment the ladies moved away from the well and drew level with us. Grushnitsky had time to strike a dramatic pose with the aid of his crutch and answered me loudly in French:

'*Mon cher, je haïs les hommes pour ne pas les mépriser, car autrement la vie serait une farce trop dégoutante.*'[31]

The pretty younger Princess turned and favoured the orator with a long gaze of curiosity. The expression of this gaze was very indefinite, but not derisive, on which I inwardly congratulated him wholeheartedly.

'This Princess Mary is very pretty indeed,' I said to him. 'She has such velvety eyes – specifically velvety: I advise you to appropriate that expression when talking about her eyes; the lower and upper lashes are so long that the sun's rays aren't reflected in her pupils. I love those eyes – without lustre: they're so soft, it's as if they're stroking you… Anyway, there only seem to be good things about her face… Well, then, does she have white teeth? That's very important! What a shame she didn't smile at your grand phrase.'

'You talk about a pretty woman as you would about an English horse,' said Grushnitsky indignantly.

'*Mon cher*,' I answered him, trying to imitate his tone, '*je méprise les femmes pour ne pas les aimer, car autrement la vie serait un mélodrame trop ridicule.*'[32]

I turned and walked away from him. For about half an hour I strolled along paths flanked by vines, over limestone cliffs and among the shrubbery that hung between them. It was getting hot, and I set off for home in a hurry. Going past the sulphate spring, I stopped by the covered gallery to take a breather in its shade, and this gave me the opportunity to witness a rather curious scene. The dramatis personae were to be found in the following positions. The middle-aged Princess was sitting on a bench in the covered gallery with the Moscow dandy, and both were preoccupied with what seemed to be a serious conversation. The young Princess, who had probably already finished drinking her final glass, was walking about pensively near the well. Grushnitsky was standing right by the well; there was nobody else on the square.

I went closer and hid around the corner of the gallery. At this point Grushnitsky had dropped his glass on the sand and was making every effort to bend down and pick it up: his injured leg was hindering him. The poor thing! What lengths he went to, leaning on his crutch, but all to no avail. His expressive face really did portray suffering.

Princess Mary saw all this better than I.

Nimbler than a bird she hopped up to him, bent down, picked up the glass and handed it to him in a movement filled with inexpressible charm; then she blushed dreadfully, glanced round at the gallery and, satisfied that her mama had seen nothing, seemed to be reassured straight away. When Grushnitsky opened his mouth to thank her she was already a long way off. A minute later she came out of the gallery with her mother and the dandy but, walking past Grushnitsky, she adopted such a prim and pompous air – she didn't even turn her head, didn't notice the passionate look with which he followed her for a long time until, after going down the hill, she disappeared among the young lime trees of the boulevard... But then her bonnet appeared fleetingly across the street; she ran in through the gates of one of Pyatigorsk's best houses. The middle-aged Princess followed her and exchanged bows with Rayevich at the gates.

Only then did the poor, passionate cadet notice my presence.

'Did you see?' he said, giving my arm a tight squeeze: 'she's simply an angel!'

'Why's that?' I asked, with an air of the purest artlessness.

'Didn't you see, then?'

'Yes, I saw: she picked up your glass. If there'd been a janitor here, he'd have done the same, and in more of a hurry too, in the hope of getting a tip. But you can quite understand her feeling sorry for you: you pulled such a dreadful face when you put your weight on your wounded leg…'

'And you weren't in the least touched, looking at her at that moment when her soul shone out in her face?…'

'No.'

I lied; but I wanted to infuriate him. I have an innate passion for contradiction; my whole life has been just a chain of sad and unsuccessful contradictions of the heart or the intellect. The presence of an enthusiast turns me stone cold, and I think frequent dealings with someone lethargic and phlegmatic would make a passionate dreamer of me. I confess, too, at that moment an unpleasant, but familiar feeling flitted lightly through my heart: that feeling was envy; I say 'envy' boldly, because I'm used to admitting everything to myself; and you'd be unlikely to find any young man who, after meeting a pretty woman who has riveted his idle attention and has then suddenly in his presence blatantly singled out another, equally unknown to her – you'd be unlikely, I say, to find any such young man (it stands to reason, one who lives in high society and is used to indulging his vanity) who wouldn't be unpleasantly affected by it.

Grushnitsky and I came down the hill in silence and walked along the boulevard past the windows of the house where our beauty had disappeared. She was sitting by a window. Grushnitsky tugged at my arm and cast her one of those opaquely tender looks that have so little effect on women. I directed my lorgnette at her and noted that his look had made her smile, and my impertinent lorgnette had made her really angry. And indeed, how dare a Caucasian army officer train his eyeglass on a Muscovite Princess?…

The doctor paid me a call this morning; his name's Werner, but he's Russian. What's surprising in that? I knew an Ivanov who was a German.

Werner's a remarkable man for many reasons. He's a sceptic and a materialist like almost all physicians, but at the same time a poet too, and a real one – always a poet in his actions and often in his words, though he's not written two lines in his life. He's studied all the vital strings of the human heart as people study the sinews of a corpse, but has never known how to exploit his knowledge: in the same way an excellent anatomist sometimes doesn't know how to cure a cold sore! In private Werner was normally mocking about his patients; but I once saw him crying over a dying soldier... He was poor and dreamed of millions, but wouldn't have taken a single extra step for money: he once told me he'd rather do a favour for an enemy than a friend, because the latter would mean selling your philanthropy, whereas hatred would only intensify in proportion to your adversary's generosity. He had a spiteful tongue: with one of his epigrams as a label, more than one good man has come to be thought of as a vulgar fool; his rivals, the envious physicians of the spas, spread a rumour that he drew caricatures of his patients – the patients were incensed and almost everyone dropped him. His friends, that is to say, all the truly decent men serving in the Caucasus, tried in vain to restore his fallen reputation.

His appearance was one of those that strike you unpleasantly at first glance, but which you subsequently like, once your eye has learnt to read in the irregular features the imprint of a well-tried and elevated soul. There have been instances of women falling madly in love with such men and not exchanging their ugliness for the beauty of the freshest and pinkest of Endymions[33]; you have to give women their due: they have an instinct for spiritual beauty; perhaps that's why people such as Werner love women so passionately.

Werner was short, thin and as weak as a child; he had one leg shorter than the other, like Byron; his head appeared huge in comparison with his body; his hair was close-cropped and the bumps on his skull, thus laid bare, would have amazed a phrenologist with their strange combination of contrasting inclinations. His small black eyes, always restless, tried to penetrate your thoughts. Taste and tidiness could be discerned in his clothes; his small, lean, sinewy hands were shown off in light yellow gloves. His frock coat, tie and waistcoat were consistently black in colour. The young men called him Mephistopheles[34]; he pretended to be angry about this nickname, but actually it flattered his vanity. We soon came to understand one another and became close acquaintances, because I'm incapable of friendship: of two friends, one is always the slave of the other, though often neither of them admits this to himself; I can't be a slave, and it's a tiring business being in command in such a case, because as well as that you need to be deceitful; and besides, I have servants and money! This is how we became close acquaintances: I met Werner in S*** amongst a numerous and noisy circle of young men; towards the end of the evening the conversation took a philosophical, metaphysical turn; there was discussion of convictions: everyone was convinced of all sorts of things.

'As far as I'm concerned, I'm convinced of only one thing…' said the doctor.

'What's that?' I asked, wanting to learn the opinion of a man who had up until then been silent.

'That sooner or later,' he replied, 'one fine morning, I shall die.'

'I'm richer than you,' I said; 'I have another conviction apart from that – namely, that one vile evening I had the misfortune to be born.'

Everyone thought we were talking nonsense, but in truth none of them had said anything cleverer than that. Thereafter we singled one another out from the crowd. The two of us would often meet together and discuss abstract subjects very seriously until we both noticed we were mutually hoodwinking one another. Then, looking one another meaningfully in the eye, as the Roman augurs – according to Cicero[35] – used to do, we'd begin to chuckle and, after a good deal of chuckling, we'd part, satisfied with our evening.

I was lying on the couch with my eyes fixed on the ceiling and my hands behind my head when Werner came up to my room. He sat down in an armchair, stood his walking stick in the corner, yawned and announced that it was getting hot outside. I replied that the flies were troubling me – and we both fell silent.

'Take note, good Doctor,' I said, 'that this world would be very dull without any fools… Just look, here we are, two intelligent men; we already know you can argue about anything endlessly and for that reason we don't argue; we know almost all one another's innermost thoughts; one word is an entire story for us; we can accurately see our every emotion through several layers of concealment. What's sad we find funny, what's funny we find depressing, and in general, if truth be told, we're pretty indifferent to everything apart from ourselves. There can therefore be no exchange of emotions and thoughts between us: we know everything about each other that we want to know, and we don't want to know any more; one thing remains – to recount the news. So won't you tell me something new?'

Exhausted by this long speech, I closed my eyes and yawned.

After some thought he replied: 'There is one idea, you know, in all your twaddle.'

'Two!' I replied.

'Tell me one, and I'll tell you the other myself.'

'All right, you begin!' I said, continuing to examine the ceiling and inwardly smiling.

'You'd like to know some details regarding one of the people who've come to take the waters, and I can even guess who you're concerned about, because they've already been asking about you over there.'

'Doctor! We positively can't have any conversations: we can read one another's souls.'

'Now the other one…'

'The other idea is this: I wanted to make you recount something; firstly, because listening is less tiring; secondly, you can't let anything slip out; thirdly, you may find out another man's secret; finally, because people as clever as you like listeners better than talkers. Now to business; what did the elder Princess Ligovskaya tell you about me?'

'You're very certain it was the elder one… and not her daughter?…'

'Absolutely convinced.'

'Why?'

'Because her daughter asked about Grushnitsky.'

'You have a great gift of understanding. She said she was sure the young man in the soldier's greatcoat had been reduced to the ranks for duelling…'

'I hope you left her with that pleasant delusion…'

'It stands to reason.'

'There's the opening!' I cried in delight; 'and we'll do what we can about the comedy's denouement. Fate is clearly taking trouble to see I'm not bored.'

'I have the feeling,' said the doctor, 'poor Grushnitsky is going to be your victim…'

'Carry on, Doctor…'

'Princess Ligovskaya said your face was familiar. I remarked to her that she'd probably met you in St Petersburg, in society somewhere… I mentioned your name… It was known to her. That episode of yours seems to have caused a lot of fuss there… The Princess started talking about your escapades, doubtless adding her own remarks to society gossip… The daughter listened curiously. In her imagination you've been made into the hero of a novel in the modern taste… I didn't contradict the Princess, although I knew she was talking nonsense.'

'A worthy friend!' I said, extending my hand to him. The doctor shook it with feeling and continued:

'I'll introduce you, if you want…'

'Oh, please!' I said, clasping my hands together; 'as if heroes are introduced! They make the acquaintance of their beloved in no other way than by saving her from certain death…'

'And do you really mean to go chasing after Princess Mary?…'

'On the contrary, quite on the contrary!… Doctor, I triumph at last, you don't understand me!… Actually, that saddens me, Doctor,' I continued after a moment's silence: 'I never reveal my secrets myself, but I really like them to be guessed, because that way I can always deny them if necessary. Anyway, you must describe mama and her daughter for me. What sort of people are they?'

'Firstly, the mother's a woman of forty-five,' replied Werner: 'her stomach's fine, but her blood's not good: she has red blotches on her cheeks. She's spent the latter half of her life in Moscow, and with her quiet life there has grown fat. She likes risqué stories and sometimes says something improper herself when her daughter's out of the room. She declared to me that her daughter is as innocent as a dove. What's it to me?… I wanted to reply that she could rest at ease, I wouldn't tell anyone about it! The Princess is here to be treated for rheumatism, and her daughter for God knows what; I told them both to drink two glasses of sulphate water a day and to bathe twice a week in a diluted bath. The mother doesn't seem to be used to giving orders; she has respect for the intelligence and knowledge of her daughter, who's read Byron in English and knows algebra: young ladies in Moscow have evidently gone in for learning, and a good thing too! Russian men are so charmless in general that flirting with them must be intolerable for a clever woman. The mother is very fond of young men; the daughter regards them with a certain contempt: a Muscovite habit! In Moscow the only nourishment they get is from forty-year-old wags.'

'And have you been to Moscow, Doctor?'

'Yes, I've practised there a little.'

'Continue.'

'Well, I think I've said everything… Oh yes! There's something else: Princess Mary seems to like talking about emotions, passions and the like… she was in St Petersburg for one winter and didn't like it, especially society: she was probably given a cold reception.'

'Did you see no one at their house today?'

'On the contrary; there was an adjutant, a tense Guards Officer and some newly arrived lady, a relative of the Princess through her husband, very pretty, but apparently very ill… Haven't you met her at the well? She's of medium height, blonde, with regular features, a consumptive complexion and a black mole on her right cheek: I was struck by the expressiveness of her face.'

'A mole!' I muttered through my teeth. 'Surely not?'

The doctor looked at me and, putting his hand on my heart, said triumphantly: 'You know her…' My heart was indeed beating harder than normal.

'Now it's your turn to be triumphant!' I said. 'But I'm relying on you: you won't betray me. I've not seen her yet, but I'm sure I recognise in your portrait a woman I used to love in days gone by… Don't say a word to her about me; if she asks, be rude about me.'

'As you wish!' said Werner, with a shrug.

When he'd gone, a terrible sadness wrung my heart. Was it fate that had brought us together again in the Caucasus, or had she come here

76

on purpose, knowing she'd meet me?... And how would we meet?... And then, was it her?... My presentiments have never deceived me. There isn't a man in the world over whom the past could have won such power as it has over me. Every reminder of bygone sorrow or joy strikes painfully into my soul and extracts from it ever the same sounds... I'm foolishly formed: I forget nothing – nothing!

After lunch, at about six o'clock, I went to the boulevard: there was a crowd of people; the two Princesses were sitting on a bench, surrounded by young men falling over one another to be charming. I positioned myself on another bench at a certain distance, stopped two officers I knew from the D. Regiment, and began telling them some story; it was evidently funny, because they began chuckling like madmen. Curiosity drew several of those surrounding Princess Mary to me; little by little every single one of them abandoned her and joined my circle. I just kept on talking: my anecdotes were clever to the point of stupidity, my mockery of eccentric passers-by was spiteful to the point of savagery... I continued entertaining my audience until the sun went down. Several times Princess Mary walked past me, arm in arm with her mother and accompanied by some lame little old man; several times her gaze, as it fell on me, expressed annoyance, while trying to express indifference...

'What was he telling you?' she asked one of the young men who returned to her out of politeness. 'It must have been a very interesting story – his feats in battle, perhaps?...' She said this quite loudly and probably with the intention of having a dig at me. 'Aha!' I thought: 'You're really angry, dear Princess; just you wait, you've seen nothing yet!'

Grushnitsky followed her like a predatory beast and didn't let her out of his sight: I bet he'll be asking somebody tomorrow to introduce him to her mother. She'll be very pleased, because she's bored.

16TH MAY

In the course of two days my affairs have moved on greatly. Princess Mary positively hates me; I've already had two or three epigrams on my account passed on to me, quite caustic, but at the same time flattering. She finds it terribly strange that I, accustomed to good society and on such close terms with her cousins and aunts in St Petersburg, don't try to make her acquaintance. We meet every day by the well, on the boulevard; I use all my powers to distract her admirers, the brilliant adjutants, the pale Muscovites and the rest – and I almost always succeed. I've always hated receiving guests: now I have a full house every day, they have lunch, dinner, they gamble – and, alas, my champagne triumphs over the power of her magnetic eyes!

Yesterday I met her in Chelakhov's shop; she was bargaining for a wonderful Persian rug. She was begging her mama not to be mean: this rug would be such an adornment for her study!... I offered an extra forty roubles and bought it over her head; for that I was rewarded with a glance in which there shone the most ravishing fury. Around lunchtime I deliberately ordered my Circassian horse to be led past her windows, covered with this rug. Werner was with them at the time and told me that the effect of this scene was most dramatic. Princess Mary wants to preach a crusade against me; I've even noticed that two adjutants already exchange very dry bows with me in her presence, yet have lunch with me every day.

Grushnitsky has adopted an air of mystery: he walks around with his hands behind his back and recognises nobody; his leg has suddenly got better: he scarcely limps. He found the opportunity to enter into conversation with Princess Ligovskaya and to pay some compliment to Princess Mary; she's evidently not very discriminating, for since then she's been replying to his bows with the sweetest of smiles.

'Do you definitely not want to make the acquaintance of the Ligovskayas?' he said to me yesterday.

'Definitely.'

'But really! It's the most pleasant house in the spa! All the best society here…'

'My friend, I'm dreadfully tired even of society that *isn't* from here. So do you call on them?'

'Not yet; I've spoken twice or more with Princess Mary, but you know, fishing for an invitation to the house is embarrassing somehow, though it is the done thing here… It'd be a different matter if I were wearing epaulettes…'

'Oh, come on! You're of far more interest like that! You simply don't know how to exploit your advantageous position... And in the eyes of every sentimental young lady your soldier's greatcoat makes you a suffering hero.'

Grushnitsky gave a smug smile.

'What nonsense!' he said.

'I'm certain,' I continued, 'the Princess is already in love with you.'

He blushed to the roots of his hair and started looking sulky.

O Vanity! You are the lever with which Archimedes wanted to lift the Earth!...[36]

'You're full of jokes!' he said, pretending to be angry. 'In the first place, she knows me so little as yet...'

'Women only love men they don't know.'

'And I don't have any pretensions to taking her fancy at all: I simply want to make the acquaintance of a pleasant house, and it would be quite ridiculous for me to have any hopes... Now you, for example, you're a different matter, you conquerors from the capital: just look at the way women melt... But do you know, Pechorin, what the Princess said about you?...'

'What? Has she already been talking to you about me?...'

'Don't start rejoicing, though. I got into conversation with her somehow at the well, by chance, and one of the first things she said was: "Who's that gentleman who has such an unpleasant, uncomfortable gaze? He was with you that time..." When she remembered her charming deed, she blushed and didn't want to mention the day. "You don't need to say which day," I answered her: "it will always be memorable for me..." Pechorin, my friend, I can't congratulate you; you're in her bad books... And it really is a shame, because Mary's very sweet!...'

It should be noted that Grushnitsky is one of those men who, when talking about a woman with whom they're scarcely acquainted, call her *my Mary*, *my Sophie*, if she's had the good fortune to take their fancy.

I adopted a serious air and answered him:

'Yes, she's not bad-looking... But beware, Grushnitsky! Young ladies in Russia live for the most part on platonic love alone, without mingling it with any thoughts of marriage; and platonic love is the most disturbing. The Princess seems to be one of those women who

79

want to be amused; if she's bored beside you two minutes running, you're irretrievably lost: your silence must arouse her curiosity, your conversation never satisfy it completely; you must alarm her at every minute; she'll publicly disregard opinion for you ten times and call this a sacrifice, and, to reward herself for it, will start tormenting you – and then she'll simply say she can't stand you. If you don't win power over her, even her first kiss won't give you any right to a second one; she'll have her fill of flirting with you, but in a couple of years she'll marry some freak out of obedience to her mama, and start assuring you that she's miserable, that she only ever loved one man – you, that is – but that Heaven didn't want to unite her with him, because he wore a soldier's greatcoat, although beneath that heavy, grey greatcoat there beat a passionate and noble heart…'

Grushnitsky banged his fist down on the table and started walking to and fro around the room.

I chuckled inwardly and even smiled a couple of times, but fortunately he didn't notice it. It's clear he's in love, because he's become even more gullible than before; he's even suddenly got a locally made silver ring with niello decoration: it seemed suspicious to me… I began examining it, and what did I find?… The name *Mary* was engraved in small letters on the inner side, and next to it – the date of the day when she picked up the famous glass. I've kept my discovery a secret; I don't want to extort admissions from him; I want him to choose me as his confidant himself – and then I'm going to enjoy myself…

I got up late today; I arrived at the well – by then there was no one there. It was getting hot; shaggy little white clouds were speeding from the snowy mountains, promising a thunderstorm; Mashuk's peak was smoking like an extinguished torch; winding and creeping around it like snakes were the grey shreds of clouds, delayed in their flight and seemingly entangled on its prickly scrub. The air was imbued with electricity. I went into the depths of a vine walk leading to a grotto; I felt sad. I was thinking of that young woman with the mole on her cheek that the doctor had told me about… Why was she here? And was it her? And why did I think it was her? And why was I even so certain of it? How many women were there with moles on their cheeks? With thoughts like that I approached the grotto. I looked: in the cool shade of its vault, on a stone bench sat a woman in a straw hat, wrapped up in a black shawl, with her head lowered onto her breast; the hat hid her face. I already meant to turn back so as not to disturb her dreams, when she glanced at me.

'Vera!' I cried involuntarily.

She gave a start and turned pale. 'I knew you were here,' she said. I sat down beside her and took her by the hand. A long-forgotten tremor ran through my veins at the sound of that sweet voice; her deep and calm eyes looked into mine: expressed in them was mistrustfulness and something resembling a reproach.

'It's been a long time since we last met,' I said.

'A long time, and we've both changed in many ways!'

'And so you don't love me any more!...'

'I'm married!...' she said.

'Again? That reason was there a few years ago too, though, and yet...'

She pulled her hand from mine and the colour flared up in her cheeks.

'Perhaps you love your second husband?...'

She didn't reply and turned away.

'Or is he very jealous?'

Silence.

'Well, then? He's young, good-looking, probably especially rich, and you're afraid...' I glanced at her and took fright; her face expressed profound despair, tears glistened in her eyes.

'Tell me,' she whispered eventually, 'is it great fun for you tormenting me? I ought to hate you. Ever since we've known one another you've brought me nothing but suffering...' Her voice began to quiver, she leant towards me and lowered her head onto my chest.

'Perhaps,' I thought, 'that's precisely why you loved me: joys get forgotten, but sorrows never...'

I held her tight and we stayed like that for a long time. Finally our lips converged and melted into a passionate, thrilling kiss; her hands were as cold as ice, her head was on fire. At this point we began one of those conversations which make no sense on paper, which can't be repeated and can't even be remembered: the significance of the sounds supplants and supplements the significance of the words, just as in Italian opera.

She definitely doesn't want me to meet her husband – that little old man with a limp I saw fleetingly on the boulevard: she married him for the sake of her son. He's rich and suffers from rheumatic pains. I didn't allow myself a single jibe at him: she respects him like a father – and is going to deceive him like a husband... The human heart in general is a strange thing, and the female one in particular!

Vera's husband, Semyon Vasilyevich G***v, is a distant relative of Princess Ligovskaya. He lives just close by her; Vera often calls on the Princess; I gave her my word to make the Ligovskayas' acquaintance and to pursue the young one so as to distract attention from her. Thus my plans haven't been upset one little bit, and I shall have some fun...

Fun!... Yes, I'm already through with that period of spiritual life when you seek only happiness, when your heart feels the need to love someone deeply and passionately: now I only want to be loved, and by a very few at that; I even think one constant attachment would be enough for me: the pitiful habit of the heart!...

One thing I've always found strange: I've never become the slave of the women I've loved; on the contrary, I've always won unassailable power over their will and heart without trying to do so at all. Why is that? Is it because I never hold anything very dear, whereas they're forever afraid they'll lose their grip on me? Or is it the magnetic influence of a powerful organism? Or have I simply never been lucky enough to meet a woman of unyielding character?

I must admit that I certainly don't love women of character: that's no business of theirs!...

It's true, I remember now, once, just the once, I did love a woman with a strong will whom I could never conquer... We parted as enemies – but even then, perhaps if I'd met her five years later we'd have parted differently...

Vera's ill, very ill, though she won't admit it; I'm afraid she might have consumption or the sickness they call *fièvre lente*[37] – not a Russian illness at all, and our language has no name for it.

The thunderstorm caught us in the grotto and detained us for half an hour more. She didn't make me swear to be faithful, didn't ask if I'd loved anyone else since we'd parted... She put herself in my hands once again with her former insouciance – and I shan't deceive her: she is the one woman in the world I wouldn't have the strength to deceive. I know we shall soon part again and perhaps for ever: we'll both take different paths to the grave; but the memory of her will remain inviolable in my soul; I've always kept telling her that, and she believes me, although she says she doesn't.

Finally we parted; I followed her with my gaze for a long time, until her hat had disappeared behind the bushes and the cliffs. My heart contracted painfully, as after a first parting. Oh, how pleased I was at that feeling! Could this be youth with its wholesome storms wanting to return to me again, or was it just its farewell glance, its final gift – as a memento?... And it's funny to think that, to look at, I'm still a boy: my face, albeit pale, is still fresh; my limbs are supple and slim; my hair curls thickly, my eyes shine, my blood's on the boil...

On returning home, I mounted up and galloped off into the steppe; I love galloping on a hot horse through the tall grass into the wind of the wilderness; I greedily gulp down the fragrant air and direct my gaze into the blue distance, trying to discern the misty outlines of objects which become clearer and clearer with every minute. No matter what grief might lie heavy on your heart, no matter what anxiety might be wearying your thoughts, all will be dispersed in a moment; your soul will find ease, physical fatigue will conquer mental disquiet. There isn't a woman's gaze I wouldn't forget at the sight of the curly-headed mountains lit by the southern sun, at the sight of the blue sky, or harking to the roar of a torrent tumbling from crag to crag.

I expect the Cossacks yawning on their *watchtowers*, when they saw me galloping needlessly and aimlessly, spent a long time fretting over this mystery, for by my clothing they probably took me for a Circassian. I've actually been told that in Circassian costume and on horseback I look more like a Kabardian than many Kabardians do. And it's quite true, so far as that noble military dress is concerned, I'm a complete dandy: not one superfluous galloon; expensive weapons with simple decoration, the fur on the hat not too long and not too short; leggings and high boots as perfect a fit as possible; a white quilted jacket and a dark brown Circassian coat. I spent a long time studying the mountaineers' seat on horseback: there's no better way of flattering my vanity than by acknowledging my skill in riding the Caucasian way. I keep four horses: one for myself, three for acquaintances, so that I don't get bored dragging across the fields on my own; people borrow my horses with pleasure but never ride with me. It was already six o'clock in the afternoon when I remembered it was time to have lunch; my horse was exhausted; I rode out onto the road leading from Pyatigorsk to the German colony[38] where spa society often rides *en piquenique*[39]. The road winds between bushes, descending into little gullies where noisy streams flow under the shelter of tall grass; towering all around like an amphitheatre are the blue hulks of Beshtu, Snake, Iron and Bald Mountains. After descending into one of these gullies, called *balky* in the local dialect, I stopped to water my horse; at this time a noisy and brilliant cavalcade appeared on the road; ladies in black and blue riding habits, cavaliers in costumes comprising a mixture of 'the Circassian and the Nizhny Novgorod'[40]; at the head rode Grushnitsky with Princess Mary.

Ladies at the spas still believe in attacks in broad daylight by Circassians; doubtless for this reason Grushnitsky had hung over the top of his soldier's greatcoat a sabre and a pair of pistols: he was quite ridiculous in these heroic vestments. A tall bush hid me from them, but I was able to see everything through its leaves and to guess from their expressions that the conversation was a sentimental one. At last they approached the descent; Grushnitsky took the rein of the Princess' horse, and then I heard the end of their conversation:

'And do you want to stay in the Caucasus all your life?' said the Princess.

'What's Russia to me?' replied her cavalier: 'A country where thousands of people will look upon me with contempt because they're richer than me, whereas here – here this heavy greatcoat didn't prevent my meeting you…'

'On the contrary…' said the Princess, blushing.

Grushnitsky's face portrayed pleasure. He continued:

'Here my life will pass noisily, unnoticed and quickly, under the bullets of savages, and if each year God were to send me one bright glance from a woman, one like the…'

At this point they drew level with me; I struck my horse with my whip and rode out from behind the bush…

'*Mon Dieu, un circassien!…*'[41] cried the Princess in horror.

To disabuse her completely I answered in French with a little bow: '*Ne craignez rien, madame – je ne suis pas plus dangereux que votre cavalier.*'[42]

She was embarrassed – but why? Because of her mistake, or because my reply seemed to her impertinent? I'd like my latter assumption to be right. Grushnitsky threw me a look of displeasure.

Late in the evening, that is to say, at about eleven o'clock, I went for a walk down the boulevard's lime avenue. The town was asleep, only in a few windows could lights be glimpsed. On three sides were the black crests of crags, offshoots of Mashuk, on whose summit lay an ominous little cloud; the moon was rising in the east; in the distance glistened the silver fringe of the snowy mountains. The calls of the sentries intermingled with the noise of the hot springs, released for the night. From time to time the resonant tread of a horse rang down the street, accompanied by the creaking of a Nogaian bullock-cart and a mournful Tatar refrain. I sat down on a bench and fell deep in thought… I felt the need to pour out my thoughts in a friendly conversation… but with whom?… 'What's Vera doing now?' I thought… I'd have given a great deal to have squeezed her hand at that moment.

Suddenly I heard rapid, uneven footsteps… Probably Grushnitsky… So it was!

'Where've you come from?' – 'Princess Ligovskaya's,' he said very pompously. 'How Mary sings!…'

'Do you know what?' I said to him: 'I bet she doesn't know you're a cadet; she thinks you've been reduced to the ranks…'

'Perhaps! What's it to me?…' he said absent-mindedly.

'No, I'm just saying…'

'But do you know you made her dreadfully angry today? She thought it was unheard-of impertinence; it was all I could do to assure her that you're so well brought up and know good society so well that you couldn't have intended to insult her; she says you have an insolent stare and must be of the very highest opinion of yourself.'

'She's not wrong… And don't you want to take her part?'

'I regret I don't yet have the right…'

'Oho!' I thought. 'He evidently already has hopes…'

'Still, it's you that's worse off,' continued Grushnitsky: 'it'll be hard for you to get to know them now – and that's a shame! It's one of the most pleasant houses I know…'

I smiled inwardly.

'The most pleasant house for me just now is my own,' I said with a yawn, and stood up to go.

'Admit it though, aren't you repentant?…'

'What nonsense! If I want, I'll be at the Princess' house in the evening tomorrow…'

'We'll see…'

'To give you pleasure, I'll even start paying court to her daughter…'

'Yes, if she wants to talk to you…'

'I'll just wait for the moment when your conversation starts to bore her… Farewell!…'

'And I'll go for a wander around – I won't be able to get to sleep now for anything… Listen, let's go to the restaurant instead, there's gambling there… I need powerful sensations today…'

'I hope you lose…'

I went home.

21ST MAY

Almost a week has passed, and I still haven't made the acquaintance of the Ligovskayas. I'm waiting for a suitable opportunity. Grushnitsky follows Princess Mary around everywhere like a shadow; their conversations are endless: so when will he start to bore her?… The mother pays no attention to it because he's *not eligible*. There's the logic of mothers! I've noticed two or three tender glances – I need to put a stop to it.

Yesterday Vera appeared at the well for the first time… Since we met in the grotto she hadn't left the house. We dipped our glasses at the same time and, while bending down, she said to me in a whisper:

'You don't want to meet the Ligovskayas! It's the only place we can see each other…'

A reproach!... How dull! But I deserved it...

Incidentally: tomorrow there's a subscription ball in the main hall of the restaurant, and I'm going to dance the mazurka with Princess Mary.

22ND MAY

The hall of the restaurant was transformed into the hall of the Nobles' Assembly Rooms. At nine o'clock everyone had gathered. Princess Ligovskaya and her daughter were among the last to appear; many of the ladies looked at Princess Mary with envy and ill will because she dresses tastefully. The ones who consider themselves the local aristocrats concealed their envy and attached themselves to her. What can be done? Wherever you have female society, an upper and a lower circle will immediately appear. Outside by the window amidst a crowd of common people stood Grushnitsky with his face pressed against the glass, never taking his eyes off his goddess; she, while walking past, gave him a scarcely perceptible nod of the head. He beamed like the sun... The dancing began with a polonaise; then they struck up a waltz. Spurs began to ring, coat-tails lifted and began whirling around.

I stood behind a fat lady, shielded by pink feathers; the volume of her dress recalled the days of farthingales, and the blotchiness of her rough skin the happy era of black taffeta beauty spots. The largest of the warts on her neck was hidden under the clasp of her necklace. She was saying to her cavalier, a captain of dragoons:

'That young Princess Ligovskaya's the most unbearable chit of a girl! Just imagine, she pushed me and failed to apologise; then, what's more, she turned around and gave me a look through her lorgnette... *C'est impayable!*...[43] And what's she got to be so haughty about? She really needs to be taught a lesson...'

'That can be arranged!' replied the obliging captain, and went off into another room.

I went up to Princess Mary straight away and invited her to waltz, exploiting the laxity of local custom, which permits you to dance with ladies you don't know.

She was scarcely able either to make herself refrain from smiling or to conceal her triumph; quite quickly, however, she managed to adopt an utterly indifferent and even severe air. She casually lowered her hand onto my shoulder, inclined her head slightly to one side, and we were off. I've not come across a more voluptuous and supple waist! Her fresh breath touched my face; a lock of hair that in the whirlwind of the waltz had become detached from its fellows would at times slip across my burning cheek... I made three circuits. (She waltzes amazingly well.) She was breathless, her eyes were glazed, her parted lips were scarcely able to whisper the obligatory: '*Merci, monsieur*.'[44]

After a few moments of silence I said to her, adopting a most submissive air:

'I've heard, Princess, that without knowing you at all, I've already had the misfortune to earn your disfavour... that you've found me impertinent... is that really true?'

'And now you'd like to confirm me in that opinion?' she replied with an ironic little grimace, which actually suits her mobile features very well.

'If I've had the impertinence to insult you in any way, permit me the even greater impertinence of asking your forgiveness... And I should truly like to prove to you that you were wrong about me...'

'You'll find that rather difficult...'

'But why?...'

'Because you don't call on us, and these balls probably won't often be repeated.'

That means, I thought, their doors are closed to me for good.

'You know, Princess,' I said, with a certain annoyance, 'a repentant criminal should never be spurned: in despair he might become twice the criminal he was before... and then...'

The chuckling and whispering of those around us forced me to turn and interrupt my phrase. Several paces away from me stood a group of men, and among them the captain of dragoons who'd expressed hostile intentions towards the charming Princess; he in particular was very pleased about something, rubbing his hands, chuckling and exchanging winks with his comrades. Suddenly from their midst emerged a gentleman in a tailcoat with long whiskers and a red face, and he directed his unsteady steps straight towards the Princess: he was drunk. Stopping in front of the embarrassed Princess and putting

88

his hands behind his back, he stared at her with his dull grey eyes and pronounced in a hoarse descant:

'*Permettez...*[45] oh, what the heck!... quite simply, I'm engaging you for the mazurka...'

'What is it you want?' she pronounced in a tremulous voice, casting an imploring glance all around. Alas, her mother was a long way off, and none of the cavaliers she knew was nearby; one adjutant seemed to see it all but hid in the crowd so as not to get mixed up in an incident.

'Well, then?' said the drunken gentleman with a wink at the captain of dragoons, who was egging him on with gestures: 'Don't you want to, then? Once again, then, I have the honour to engage you *pour mazure...*[46] Perhaps you think I'm drunk? That's all right!... A lot freer, I can assure you...'

I could see she was about to faint in terror and indignation.

I went up to the drunken gentleman, took him quite firmly by the arm and, staring him in the eye, requested him to withdraw – because, I added, the Princess had promised long before to dance the mazurka with me.

'Well, nothing for it!... Another time!' he said with a laugh, and withdrew to his shamefaced comrades, who led him off straight away into the other room.

I was rewarded with an intense, wonderful gaze.

The Princess went over to her mother and told her everything; the latter found me in the throng and thanked me. She informed me that she had known my mother and was friends with half a dozen of my aunts.

'I don't know how it's come about that we've not met until now,' she added: 'but you must admit that you alone are to blame: you avoid everyone so, it's quite unheard of. I hope the air of my drawing room will dispel your spleen... Don't you think so?'

I answered her with one of those phrases that everyone should have prepared for such an instance.

The quadrilles dragged on for a dreadfully long time.

At last the mazurka rang out from the musicians' gallery; Princess Mary and I sat ourselves down.

I didn't once allude either to the drunken gentleman, or to my previous behaviour, or to Grushnitsky. The impression made on her by the unpleasant scene was bit by bit diffused; her little face bloomed; she joked very sweetly; her conversation was sharp-witted, without having any pretension to wit, lively and fluent; her remarks at times profound... With a very convoluted phrase I gave her to understand that I had liked her for some time. She inclined her head and blushed a little.

'You're a strange man!' she said with a forced laugh when she had raised her velvety eyes.

'I didn't want to make your acquaintance,' I continued, 'because you're surrounded by too dense a throng of admirers, and I was afraid I'd disappear in it completely.'

'You were wrong to be afraid! They're all very boring...'

'All of them? Surely not all?'

She looked at me intently, as though trying to remember something, then once again blushed a little and finally pronounced decisively: '*All!*'

'Even my friend Grushnitsky?'

'Is he your friend, then?' she said, displaying some doubt.

'Yes.'

'Of course, he doesn't belong to the boring category...'

'But to the unfortunate category,' I said with a laugh.

'Of course! Do you find it funny, then? I'd like to see you in his place...'

'Why, I was a cadet myself once, and, to be honest, they were the best days of my life!'

'Is he a cadet, then?' she said quickly, and then added: 'But I thought...'

'You thought what?...'

'Nothing!... Who's that lady?'

At this point the conversation changed direction and didn't return to this topic again.

Then the mazurka ended and we took our final leave of each other – until our next meeting. The ladies left... I went to have dinner and met Werner.

'Aha!' he said. 'So there you are! The one who wanted to meet the Princess only by saving her from certain death.'

'I did better,' I answered him, 'I saved her from fainting at a ball!…'
'What do you mean? Tell me!…'
'No, work it out – you who can work out anything on earth!'

23RD MAY

Around seven o'clock in the evening I was taking a walk on the boulevard. When he saw me from a distance, Grushnitsky came up to me: a ridiculous sort of rapture shone in his eyes. He clasped my hand tightly and said in a tragic voice:

'I'm grateful to you, Pechorin… You understand me?…'

'No; but it's not worth gratitude in any case,' I replied, certainly not having any good deed on my conscience.

'What do you mean? What about yesterday? You can't have forgotten?… Mary told me everything…'

'What's this? Do you share everything now, then? Gratitude too?…'

'Listen,' said Grushnitsky very pompously: 'don't make fun of my love, if you want to remain my friend… You see, I love her madly… and I think, I hope, she loves me too… I've got a request for you: you'll pay them a visit this evening; promise me you'll take note of everything; I know you're experienced in these things, you know women better than I do… Women, women! Who can understand them? Their smiles contradict their looks, their words promise and beckon, while the sound of their voice repulses… First they comprehend and divine our most secret thoughts in a moment, then they can't understand our clearest hints… Take the Princess, for example: yesterday her eyes burnt with passion when they rested on me, today they're dull and cold…'

'Perhaps it results from the effect of the waters,' I replied.

'You see the bad side to everything… materialist!' he added scornfully. 'Still, let's discuss some other material,' and, pleased with the bad pun, he cheered up.

After eight o'clock we set off together for Princess Ligovskaya's.

Passing by Vera's windows, I saw her by a window. We threw each other a rapid glance. She entered the Ligovskayas' drawing room soon after us. The Princess said she was her relative when introducing me to her. Tea was drunk; there were a lot of guests; the conversation was general. I tried to get Princess Ligovskaya to like me, joked and made her laugh wholeheartedly several times; more than once her daughter wanted to chuckle too, but she restrained herself so as not to abandon the role she'd taken on: she thinks languor suits her – and she's perhaps not wrong. Grushnitsky seems very glad she's not infected by my cheeriness.

After the tea everyone went into the reception hall.

'Are you satisfied with my obedience, Vera?' I said as I went past her.

She threw me a glance filled with love and gratitude. I'm used to those glances; but there was a time when they constituted bliss for me. Princess Ligovskaya sat her daughter down at the fortepiano; everyone asked her to sing something – I remained silent and, exploiting the commotion, moved away towards a window with Vera, who wanted to tell me something very important for both of us… It turned out to be nonsense…

Meanwhile, my indifference was annoying Princess Mary, as I was able to guess from one angry, flashing glance… Oh, I have an astonishing understanding of this conversation, dumb yet expressive, brief yet powerful!…

She began to sing: her voice isn't bad, but her singing's poor… still, I wasn't listening. Whereas Grushnitsky leant on the piano opposite her and devoured her with his eyes, continually mouthing: '*Charmant! Délicieux!*'[47] under his breath.

'Listen,' Vera said to me, 'I don't want you to meet my husband, but you must get Princess Ligovskaya to like you without fail; it's easy for you: you can do anything you want. We'll see one another only here…'

'Only?…'

She blushed and continued:

'You know I'm your slave, I never did know how to resist you… and I shall be punished for it: you'll stop loving me! At least I want to preserve my reputation… not for myself: you know that very well!… Oh, I beg you: don't torment me like before with unfounded doubts and feigned coldness: I may die soon, I feel I'm growing weaker by the day… and regardless of that, I can't think of any future life, I think only of you… You men don't understand the pleasure of a gaze, a handshake... but I, I swear to you, when I listen to your voice, I feel such profound, strange bliss that the most passionate kisses can't substitute for it.'

Meanwhile, Princess Mary had stopped singing. A murmur of praise rang out around her; I went up to her after everyone else and said something rather off-handed to her regarding her voice.

She pulled a face, poking out her lower lip, and dropped a very sarcastic curtsy.

'That's all the more flattering for me,' she said, 'since you weren't listening to me at all; but perhaps you don't like music?...'

'On the contrary... especially after lunch.'

'Grushnitsky's right when he says you have the most prosaic tastes... and I see you like music in a gastronomic context...'

'You're wrong again: I'm not a gastronome at all: I've got a very poor stomach. But music after lunch puts you to sleep, and it's healthy to sleep after lunch: therefore I like music in a medical context. Whereas in the evening, on the contrary, it irritates my nerves too much; I become either too sad or too merry. Both the one and the other are tiring when there's no positive reason to be sad or happy; and, besides, sadness in company is ridiculous, and too much merriment is unseemly...'

She didn't hear me out, went off and sat down beside Grushnitsky, and some sort of sentimental conversation began between them: the Princess, although she tried to show that she was listening to him attentively, seemed to be replying to his wise phrases rather absent-mindedly and inappropriately, because he looked at her in surprise at times, trying to guess the reason for the inner agitation that was at times portrayed in her uneasy glance...

But I've worked you out, dear Princess, beware! You want to pay me back in my own coin, prick my vanity – you won't succeed! And if you declare war on me, I'll be merciless.

In the course of the evening I deliberately tried to intervene in their conversation several times, but she greeted my remarks rather drily, and I finally withdrew in feigned annoyance. The Princess was exultant; Grushnitsky too. Be exultant, my friends, make haste... you won't be exultant for long!... What's to be done? I have a premonition... When meeting a woman, I've always divined unerringly whether she was going to love me or not…

I spent the remainder of the evening beside Vera, and talked about the old days to my heart's content… Why she loves me so, I really don't know! Particularly as she is the one woman who has understood me completely, with all my little weaknesses, nasty passions… Is evil really so attractive?…

Grushnitsky and I left together; outside he took me by the arm and, after a long silence, said:

'Well, then?'

'You're stupid,' I wanted to answer him, but I restrained myself and only shrugged my shoulders.

29TH MAY

All these days I haven't once deviated from my system. Princess Mary is beginning to like my conversation; I've told her about some of the strange incidents in my life, and she's beginning to see me as an extraordinary person. I mock everything on earth, especially feelings: it's beginning to frighten her. She doesn't dare launch into sentimental discussion with Grushnitsky in front of me, and has already replied several times to his outbursts with a mocking smile, but every time Grushnitsky goes up to her, I adopt a meek look and leave the two of them alone; the first time she was pleased at this, or tried to pretend she was; the second time she got angry with me; the third time – with Grushnitsky.

'You have very low self-esteem!' she said to me yesterday. 'Why do you think I enjoy myself more with Grushnitsky?'

I replied that for the happiness of a friend I was sacrificing my own pleasure…

'Mine too,' she added.

I looked at her intently and adopted a serious air. And then I didn't say a word to her for the whole day… In the evening she was pensive; this morning at the well even more pensive. When I went up to her, she was listening absent-mindedly to Grushnitsky, who was apparently rhapsodising over nature, but as soon as she caught sight of me, she began chuckling (very inopportunely), while pretending not to notice me. I moved away a little and began furtively watching her: she turned away from her companion and yawned twice. She's definitely tired of Grushnitsky. I shan't talk to her for another two days.

I often wonder why I'm so persistent about winning the love of a young girl I don't want to seduce and will never marry? What's the point of this feminine coquetry? Vera loves me more than Princess Mary will ever do; if she seemed to me an unassailable beauty, perhaps I'd be fascinated by the difficulty of the enterprise…

But nothing of the sort! And so it's not that restless demand for love that torments us in the first years of our youth, that tosses us from one woman to another until we find one who can't stand us; at that point our constancy begins – a true, endless passion that can be expressed mathematically by a line stretching from a point into space; the secret of this endlessness lies only in the impossibility of achieving the aim, that is, the end.

What makes me go to the trouble? Envy of Grushnitsky? The poor thing! He's not at all worthy of it. Or is it a consequence of that unpleasant, but unconquerable feeling that makes us destroy the sweet delusions of someone close to us in order to have the petty pleasure of telling him, when he asks despairingly what he ought to believe:

'My friend, it was the same with me! And as you can see, I have lunch and dinner nonetheless, and sleep very soundly, and hope I'll manage to die without tears and lamentations!'

But still there is unbounded enjoyment in possessing a young soul that has scarcely blossomed out! It's like a flower whose finest scent evaporates at the approach of the first ray of the sun; it needs to be picked at that moment and, when you've had your fill of breathing it in, thrown by the wayside: perhaps somebody else will pick it up. I sense in myself that insatiable greed which absorbs everything encountered on my way: I look at the sufferings and joys of others only in relation to myself, as nourishment that sustains my spiritual powers. I'm no longer capable of behaving like a madman under the influence of passion myself; my ambition has been crushed by circumstances, but it is manifest in a different form, for ambition is nothing other than the thirst for power, and my number one pleasure is to subordinate everything that surrounds me to my will; to arouse towards myself feelings of love, devotion and fear – isn't that the first sign and the greatest triumph of power? To be the cause of someone's suffering and joy, without having any positive right to be so – isn't that the sweetest nourishment for our pride? And what is happiness? Satiated pride. If I considered myself better, mightier than anyone else on earth, I'd be happy; if everybody loved me, I'd find within myself endless springs of love. Evil engenders evil; your first suffering gives you some conception of the pleasure of tormenting another person; the idea of evil cannot enter a man's head without his wanting to apply it to the real world: ideas are organic creations, somebody said: their birth already gives them form, and that form is action; the man who has more ideas born in his head acts more than others; for this reason a genius chained to a clerk's chair must die or go mad, in just the same way as a man with a powerful build, if he leads a sedentary life and behaves modestly, dies of an apoplectic fit.

Passions are nothing other than ideas in their first stage of develop-ment: they're the property of a youthful heart, and anyone who thinks he'll be disturbed by them all his life is a fool: many calm rivers begin as noisy waterfalls, but there isn't a single one that leaps and foams right down to the sea. Yet this calmness is often a sign of great, albeit hidden strength; fullness and depth of feelings and thoughts don't allow mad impulses: the soul, in suffering and delight, accounts sternly to itself for everything and convinces itself that that's how it should be; it knows that without storms the constant intense heat of the sun will dry it up; it's permeated with its own life – it coddles and punishes itself like a favourite child. Only in this highest state of self-knowledge can a man evaluate God's justice.

Reading over this page, I notice I've digressed a long way from my subject... But it doesn't matter... After all, I'm writing this journal for myself, and consequently everything I toss into it will, in time, be a valuable memory for me.

Grushnitsky appeared and threw his arms around my neck – he's been made an officer. We had some champagne. Dr Werner came up after him.

'I don't congratulate you,' he said to Grushnitsky.

'Why not?'

'Because the private's greatcoat suits you very well, and, you must admit, an infantry tunic made here in the spa won't give you any added interest... You see, you were an exception before, but now you'll be subject to the general rule.'

'Just keep talking, Doctor! You won't stop me feeling pleased. He doesn't know,' added Grushnitsky into my ear, 'how much hope the epaulettes have given me... O epaulettes, epaulettes! Your little stars, your little guiding stars... No! I'm completely happy now.'

'Are you coming with us on the walk to the chasm?' I asked him.

'Me? I'm not showing myself to the Princess for anything until my uniform's ready.'

'Do you want your good news announced to her?'

'No, please don't say anything... I want to surprise her...'

'Tell me though, how are things between you?'

He became embarrassed and pensive: he wanted to boast, to lie, but he was conscience-stricken, and yet at the same time he was ashamed to admit the truth.

'What do you think, does she love you?...'

'Does she love me? Please, Pechorin, what sort of ideas do you have?... So soon, how could it be?... And even if she does love me, a respectable woman wouldn't say so...'

'All right! And in your view, a respectable man presumably ought to keep quiet about his passion too?...'

'Ah, my good fellow, there's a way of doing everything! There's a lot that isn't spoken but can be deduced...'

'That's true... But the love we read in the eyes doesn't commit a woman to anything, whereas words... Beware, Grushnitsky, she's deceiving you...'

'She?...' he replied, raising his eyes to the sky and smiling smugly. 'I feel sorry for you, Pechorin!...'

He left.

In the evening a large party set off on foot for the chasm.

In the opinion of local scholars, this chasm is nothing other than an extinct crater; it's found on the slopes of Mashuk, a kilometre from town. A narrow track leads to it between bushes and cliffs; clambering up a slope, I gave my arm to the Princess, and she didn't relinquish it for the whole of the walk.

Our conversation began with some malicious talk: I started working through our acquaintances, present and absent, pointing out first their ridiculous, and then their bad sides. My bile got stirred up, I began in jest – and ended in sincere malice. Initially it amused her, but then she took fright.

'You're a dangerous man!' she said to me: 'I'd rather be at the mercy of a murderer's knife in a forest than your tongue… Quite seriously: when you decide to speak badly of me, please, better take a knife and kill me – I don't think you'll find it very hard.'

'Do I really look like a murderer?'

'You're worse…'

I stopped and thought for a moment, and then said, adopting a deeply touched look:

'Yes, such has been my lot ever since I was a child! Everyone read in my face the signs of bad characteristics which weren't there; but they were assumed – and they were born. I was shy – I was accused of slyness: I became secretive. I had a deep sense of good and evil; nobody showed me affection, everyone insulted me: I became vindictive; I was gloomy – other children are cheerful and talkative; I felt myself superior to them – I was put down as inferior. I became envious. I was ready to love the whole world – nobody understood me: and I learnt to hate. My colourless youth passed in a struggle with myself and the world: my finest feelings, fearing mockery, I buried in the depths of my heart: and there they died. I told the truth – I wasn't believed: I became deceitful; after getting to know the world and the mainsprings of society, I became an expert in the science of life and saw how others were happy without any expertise, enjoying for nothing the advantages for which I had so tirelessly strived. And then in my heart despair was born – not the despair that's cured through the barrel of a pistol, but a cold, impotent despair, concealed with civility and a genial smile. I became a moral cripple: one half of my soul didn't exist, it had dried up, evaporated, died, I had cut it off and thrown it away – while the other half stirred and lived at the service of everyone, and yet nobody noticed, because nobody knew of the existence of its other lost half; but now you've awakened within me a memory of it, and I've read you its epitaph. All epitaphs in general seem ridiculous to many, but not to me, especially when I remember what lies beneath them. Still, I'm not asking you to share my opinion: if my outburst seems ridiculous to you – please, do laugh: I can tell you in advance, it won't distress me in the least.'

At that moment I met her eyes: there were tears moving in them, and her arm, leaning on mine, was trembling; her cheeks were aglow, she felt sorry for me! Compassion, a feeling to which all women submit so easily, had sunk its claws into her inexperienced heart. Throughout the entire walk she was absent-minded, flirted with no one – and that's a great sign!

We arrived at the chasm; the ladies abandoned their cavaliers, but she didn't relinquish my arm. The witticisms of the local dandies didn't make her laugh; the steepness of the precipice by which she stood didn't frighten her, whereas the other young ladies squealed and closed their eyes.

On the way back I didn't renew our sad conversation; but she replied to my frivolous questions and jokes briefly and absent-mindedly.

'Have you been in love?' I asked her finally.

She gave me an intent look, shook her head, and again fell deep in thought: it was clear she wanted to say something, but she didn't know how to begin; her breast was heaving... What can you do? A muslin sleeve is a weak defence, and a spark of electricity ran from my arm to hers; almost all passions begin like that, and we often deceive ourselves greatly, thinking a woman loves us for our physical or moral attributes; of course, they prepare, predispose their hearts to receive the sacred fire, but all the same, it's the first touch that decides the matter.

'I've been very amiable today, haven't I?' the Princess said to me with a forced smile when we returned from the walk.

We parted.

She's displeased with herself; she's accusing herself of coldness... Oh, this is the first, the most important triumph! Tomorrow she'll want to compensate me. I know it all off by heart – that's the boring part!

I saw Vera today. She wore me out with her jealousy. The Princess seems to have taken it into her head to confide the secrets of her heart to her; it must be admitted, a happy choice!

'I can guess where it's all leading,' Vera said to me. 'Better simply tell me now that you love her.'

'But if I don't love her?'

'Then why on earth pursue her, why alarm and disturb her imagination?... Oh, how well I know you! Listen, if you want me to believe you, come to Kislovodsk in a week's time! We're moving there the day after tomorrow. The Princess is staying on longer here. Rent an apartment nearby; we'll be staying in the big house near the spring, on the mezzanine; Princess Ligovskaya is downstairs, and nearby is a house belonging to the same owner that isn't yet taken... Will you come?...'

I promised – and sent this very day for the apartment to be taken.

Grushnitsky came to see me at six o'clock in the evening and announced that his uniform would be ready tomorrow, just in time for the ball.

'At last I shall dance with her for an entire evening... And I'll talk all I want!' he added.

'And when's the ball?'

'Tomorrow, of course! Don't you know, then? It's a big event, and the local authorities have taken on the organisation...'

'Let's go to the boulevard...'

'Not for anything, not in this disgusting greatcoat...'

'What, don't you like it any more?...'

I left alone and, meeting Princess Mary, invited her to dance the mazurka. She seemed surprised and pleased.

'I thought you only danced out of necessity, like last time,' she said, smiling very sweetly...

She doesn't seem to notice Grushnitsky's absence at all.

'You'll be pleasantly surprised tomorrow,' I told her.

'By what?'

'It's a secret... you'll work it out yourself at the ball.'

I ended the evening at Princess Ligovskaya's; there were no guests apart from Vera and an extremely amusing little old man. I was in good spirits and improvised various extraordinary stories; Princess Mary sat opposite me and listened to my nonsense with such deep, concentrated, even tender attention that I began to feel ashamed. Where were her vivacity, her flirtatiousness, her whims, her impertinent expression, contemptuous smile, absent-minded glance?…

Vera noted it all: her sickly face portrayed deep sadness; she sat in the shadow by the window, sunk into a wide armchair… I began to feel sorry for her…

Then I told the whole dramatic story of our acquaintance, of our love – disguising it all, naturally, with invented names.

I depicted my tenderness, my anxieties and raptures so vividly, I represented her conduct and character in such an advantageous light that, like it or not, she had to forgive me my flirting with the Princess.

She rose, came and sat with us, livened up… and only at two o'clock in the morning did we remember that the doctors order us to go to bed at eleven.

5TH JUNE

Half an hour before the ball Grushnitsky came to see me in the full radiance of an infantry uniform. A bronze chain was attached to the third button, and from it hung a double lorgnette; epaulettes of unbelievable size curved upwards, looking like Cupid's little wings; his boots squeaked; in his left hand he held brown kid gloves and his cap, while with his right he continually fluffed up his waved quiff into tight curls. Self-satisfaction, and at the same time a certain lack of confidence were portrayed on his face; his festive appearance, his proud step would have made me burst out laughing had that been in accordance with my intentions.

He tossed the cap and gloves onto the table and began tugging down his tails and smartening himself up in front of the mirror; a huge black kerchief, wound onto the highest of linings, the bristles of which were supporting his chin, poked out two centimetres above his collar; to him this seemed insufficient: he pulled it up to his ears; this hard work – for the tunic collar was very tight and uncomfortable – made his face all flushed.

'They say you've been chasing after my Princess something rotten all these days?' he said, quite casually and without looking at me.

'Where are we fools to have tea, then?' I answered him, repeating a favourite saying of one of the most cunning rakes of past times, of whom Pushkin once sang.[48]

'Now tell me, is the uniform a good fit? Oh, that wretched Jew!... How it cuts into my armpits!... Do you have any scent?'

'Heavens, why do you want more? You reek of rose pomade as it is...'

'Never mind. Give it here...'

He poured half a flask down the inside of his tie, onto his handkerchief, onto his sleeves.

'Are you going to dance?' he asked.

'I don't think so.'

'I'm worried the Princess and I will have to lead the mazurka – I hardly know a single figure...'

'Have you asked her for the mazurka?'

'Not yet...'

'Mind nobody pre-empts you...'

'Indeed?' he said, striking himself on the forehead. 'Farewell... I'll go and wait for her by the entrance.' He grabbed his cap and ran off.

Half an hour later I set off as well. The street was dark and empty; around the Assembly Rooms or inn, whichever you prefer, was a crowd of people; its windows were lit up; the evening breeze carried the sounds of the regimental band to me. I walked slowly; I felt sad... Is it really my sole purpose on earth, I thought, to destroy the hopes of others? All the time I've been alive and active, fate has somehow always led me to the denouement of other people's dramas, as though without me nobody could either die or fall into despair! I've been the essential character in the fifth act, like it or not I've played the wretched role of executioner or traitor. What aim has fate had in this?... Has it appointed me to be an author of lower-class tragedies and family novels, or a collaborator with someone purveying stories to, say, *The Library for Reading*[49]?... Who's to know?... How many people, beginning their lives, think they'll end them like Alexander the Great or Lord Byron, but then remain titular councillors[50] an entire lifetime?...

Going up into the hall, I hid amongst a crowd of men and began making my observations. Grushnitsky was standing beside the Princess and saying something very heatedly; she was listening to him absent-mindedly, looking from side to side with her fan pressed against her lips; impatience was portrayed on her face, her eyes were searching all around for somebody; I quietly approached from behind to eavesdrop on their conversation.

'You're torturing me, Princess,' said Grushnitsky. 'You've changed dreadfully while I've not been seeing you…'

'You've changed too,' she replied, throwing him a quick glance, in which he failed to see the hidden mockery.

'Me? I've changed?… Oh, never! You know that's impossible! Whoever has seen you once will carry your divine image away with him for ever…'

'Stop it…'

'Why is it you don't want to listen now to things you paid gracious heed to so often, and not so long ago either?…'

'Because I don't like repetition,' she replied, laughing…

'Oh, I was sorely mistaken!… Like a madman I thought these epaulettes at least would give me the right to hope… No, better if I'd stayed my whole life in that contemptible private's greatcoat, to which I'm perhaps obliged for your attention…'

'The greatcoat really does suit you much better…'

At this point I went up and bowed to the Princess; she blushed a little and quickly said:

'Isn't it the case, Monsieur Pechorin, that the grey greatcoat suits Monsieur Grushnitsky much better?…'

'I don't agree with you,' I replied. 'In his tunic he looks even younger.'

Grushnitsky couldn't take this blow; like all boys, he has pretensions to being an old man; he thinks the deep traces of passions are a substitute for the imprint of years on his face. He threw me a furious glance, stamped his foot and moved away.

'But you must admit,' I said to the Princess, 'that although he was always quite ridiculous, not so long ago you still found him interesting… in the grey greatcoat?…'

She lowered her eyes and didn't reply.

Grushnitsky haunted the Princess the whole evening, danced either with her or vis-à-vis; he devoured her with his eyes, sighed and plagued her with entreaties and reproaches. At the end of the third quadrille she already hated him.

'I didn't expect this from you,' he said, coming up to me and taking me by the arm.

'What?'

'Are you dancing the mazurka with her?' he asked, in a triumphant voice. 'She's admitted it to me...'

'Well, what of it? Is it a secret, then?'

'It stands to reason... I should have expected it from a chit of a girl... from a flirt... But I'll have my revenge!'

'Blame it on your greatcoat or on your epaulettes, but why blame her? Why is it her fault if she no longer likes you?...'

'But then why give me hopes?'

'But then why did you have hopes? Wanting and trying to get something – that I understand, but who on earth has hopes?'

'You've won the bet – only not entirely,' he said, with a malicious smile.

The mazurka began. Grushnitsky chose no one but the Princess, the other cavaliers chose her continually: it was clearly a conspiracy against me; so much the better: she wants to talk with me, they're preventing her – she'll want to twice as much.

A couple of times I squeezed her hand; the second time she pulled it away without saying a word.

'I'm going to sleep badly tonight,' she told me, when the mazurka had come to an end.

'Grushnitsky's to blame for that.'

'Oh no!' And her face became so pensive, so sad, that I promised myself I would kiss her hand this evening without fail.

People began leaving. Helping the Princess into her carriage, I quickly pressed her little hand to my lips. It was dark, and nobody could have seen it.

I went back into the hall very pleased with myself.

The young men were having dinner at a big table, and Grushnitsky among them. When I entered, everyone fell silent: they'd evidently been talking about me. A lot of people are peeved with me after the last ball, especially the captain of dragoons, and now there definitely seems to be a hostile gang forming against me under the command of Grushnitsky. He looks so proud and courageous…

I'm very glad; I love enemies, though not in the Christian way. They amuse me, they stir my blood. To be always on your guard, to catch every glance, the significance of every word, to guess intentions, foil conspiracies, to pretend to be deceived, then suddenly with one push to overturn the whole of an enormous and painstakingly constructed edifice of cunning and scheming – that's what I call life.

Throughout dinner Grushnitsky was whispering and exchanging winks with the captain of dragoons.

6TH JUNE

This morning Vera left with her husband for Kislovodsk. I met their carriage while on my way to Princess Ligovskaya's. She nodded to me: there was reproach in her look.

But who's to blame? Why doesn't she want to give me the chance to meet with her in private? Love, like a fire, dies away without nourishment. Maybe jealousy will do what my requests couldn't.

I sat a good hour at Princess Ligovskaya's. Mary stayed in her room – she's unwell. She wasn't on the boulevard this evening. The newly formed gang, armed with lorgnettes, adopted a thoroughly threatening air. I'm glad the Princess is unwell: they'd have done something discourteous to her. Grushnitsky has tousled hair and a desperate look; he really does seem distressed, his vanity's hurt in particular; but after all, there are those in whom even despair is amusing!…

When I returned home, I noticed I was missing something. *I haven't seen her! She's unwell!* I haven't actually fallen in love with her, have I?… What nonsense!

7TH JUNE

At eleven o'clock in the morning, an hour at which Princess Ligovskaya is normally sweating in the Ermolovskaya Bath, I was walking past her house. Princess Mary was sitting pensively by the window; on seeing me, she leapt up.

I went up into the entrance hall; there were no servants about, and, exploiting the freedom of local manners, I stole through into the drawing room unannounced.

A dull pallor covered the Princess' sweet face. She was standing by the fortepiano with one hand leaning on the back of an armchair: that hand was trembling a tiny bit; I went up to her quietly and said:

'Are you angry with me?...'

She directed her languorous, profound gaze up at me and shook her head; her lips tried to say something, but couldn't; her eyes filled with tears; she dropped into the armchair and covered her face with her hands.

'What's wrong with you?' I said, taking her by the hand.

'You don't respect me!... Oh, leave me alone!...'

I took several steps... She straightened up in the armchair and her eyes flashed...

Taking hold of the door handle, I stopped and said:

'Forgive me, Princess! I acted like a madman... It won't happen a second time: I shall take my own measures... Why should you need to know what's been happening in my soul up until now? You'll never learn of it, and so much the better for you. Farewell.'

As I was leaving, I think I heard her crying.

I wandered on foot in the environs of Mashuk until evening, got dreadfully tired and, arriving home, threw myself down on the bed in utter exhaustion.

Werner dropped in on me.

'Is it true,' he asked, 'that you're marrying Princess Ligovskaya's daughter?'

'Why?'

'The whole town's talking: all my invalids are preoccupied with this important item of news, and those invalids are the sort of people who know everything!'

'This is Grushnitsky's doing!' I thought.

'To prove to you, Doctor, the falsity of these rumours, I can tell you in confidence that tomorrow I'm moving to Kislovodsk...'

'And Princess Ligovskaya too?...'

'No; she's staying here for another week...'

'So you're not getting married?...'

'Doctor, Doctor! Look at me: do I really look like a bridegroom, or anything else of the sort?'

'I'm not saying that... But you know, there are instances...' he added, with a sly smile, 'in which a noble man is obliged to get married, and there are mamas who at the very least don't prevent those instances... So I advise you as a close acquaintance to be more careful. The air here at the spas is highly dangerous: how many fine young men, worthy of a better fate, have I seen leaving here to go straight to the altar... Would you believe it, someone even tried to marry me off? To be precise, it was a provincial mama whose daughter was very pale. I had the misfortune to tell her that her complexion would return after her wedding; with tears of gratitude she then offered me her daughter's hand and her entire fortune – fifty serfs, I think. But I replied that I was incapable of it...'

Werner left in the complete certainty that he'd forewarned me.

From what he said I noted that various nasty rumours have already been spread around town about Princess Mary and me: Grushnitsky will pay for this!

10TH JUNE

And so it's already three days I've been in Kislovodsk. Every day I see Vera at the well and out walking. Waking up in the morning, I take a seat by the window and train my lorgnette on her balcony; she's already been dressed for a long time and is waiting for the agreed signal; we meet as if by accident in the garden that descends from our houses towards the well. The bracing mountain air has returned the colour to her face and her strength. Not for nothing is Narzan called 'the warrior's spring'. The local residents claim that the air in Kislovodsk predisposes you to love, that the denouements of all the romances that ever began at the foot of Mashuk take place here. And indeed, everything here breathes seclusion; everything here is mysterious – the dense canopies of the lime walks, bending over the torrent that cuts itself a path amongst the greenery of the mountains, roaring and foaming as it falls from one slab of rock to another; the gorges, filled with shadows and silence, which branch off in all directions from here; the freshness of the aromatic air, heavy with the fragrance of tall southern grasses and white acacia – and the constant, sweetly soporific noise of the ice-cold streams, which, upon meeting at the end of the valley, chase after one another amicably, and finally hurl themselves into the Podkumok. On this side the gorge is wider and turns into a green depression; along it winds a dusty road. Each time I look at it, I always imagine a carriage is coming and a little pink face is peeping out of the carriage window. A good many carriages have travelled down this road already – but that one still hasn't. The suburb outside the fort has become well populated; in the restaurant built on the hill, just a few paces from my apartment, lights are beginning to be glimpsed through the double line of poplars in the evening; noise and the clinking of glasses ring out late into the night.

Nowhere is so much Kakhetian wine or mineral water drunk as here.

> *Though these two occupations to combine*
> *In many the desire is strong – it isn't mine.*[51]

Every day Grushnitsky gets rowdy at the inn with his gang and scarcely bows to me.

He arrived only yesterday, but has already managed to quarrel with three old men who wanted to get into the bath before him: misfortunes certainly develop a bellicose spirit in him.

11TH JUNE

They've finally arrived. I was sitting by the window when I heard the clatter of their carriage: my heart leapt... What's this, then? I'm not in love, am I?... I'm so stupidly made that it might be expected of me.

I had lunch with them. Princess Ligovskaya looks at me very tenderly and doesn't stray away from her daughter... that's bad! But on the other hand, Vera's jealous of Princess Mary and me: so I've succeeded in achieving that fortunate position! What will a woman not do to distress her rival? I remember there was one who fell in love with me because I loved someone else. There's nothing more paradoxical than the female mind: it's hard to convince women of anything, you need to bring them to the point where they convince themselves; the sequence of proofs with which they destroy their prejudices is very original; to master their dialectic, you have to overturn in your mind all the rules of logic learnt in school. For example, the normal process is:

'This man loves me; but I'm married: therefore, I shouldn't love him.'

The female process is:

'I shouldn't love him, since I'm married: but he loves me – therefore…'

There are several dots here, since Reason no longer says anything, and for the most part the talking is done by the tongue, the eyes and, following them, the heart, if the woman has one.

What if these notes ever catch a woman's eye? – 'Calumny!' she'll cry in indignation.

Ever since poets have been writing and women reading them (for which the deepest gratitude), they've been called angels so many times that they really have, in their simplicity of soul, come to believe that compliment, forgetting that those same poets eulogised Nero as a demigod in return for money…

I would be an inappropriate one to talk about them so maliciously – I, who haven't loved anything on earth apart from them – I, who have always been prepared to sacrifice my tranquillity, my ambition, my life for them… But then I'm not trying in a fit of annoyance and injured vanity to strip away from them the magical veil that only an accustomed gaze can penetrate. No, everything I say about them is merely a consequence of:

> *The mind's cold-blooded observations,*
> *The heart's disconsolate remarks.*[52]

Women should wish that all men knew them as well as I do, because I've loved them a hundred times more since I stopped being afraid of them and grasped their little weaknesses.

Incidentally, the other day Werner compared women to the enchanted forest that Tasso talks about in his *Jerusalem Delivered*.[53] 'Just approach,' he said, 'and such horrors come flying at you from all directions that God preserve you: duty, pride, respectability, public opinion, mockery, scorn… You don't have to look, but just keep going straight on; little by little the monsters disappear, and there opens up before you a quiet and bright glade, in the middle of which a green myrtle is blooming. But woe betide if, at the first steps, your heart should falter and you should turn back!'

12TH JUNE

This evening was rich in events. About three kilometres from Kislovodsk, in the gorge through which the Podkumok flows, there's a cliff called *The Ring*; it's a portal formed by nature; it soars up on a high hill, and through it the setting sun casts its final, fiery glance at the world. A numerous cavalcade set off for it to look at the sunset through the window of stone. None of us, to tell the truth, was thinking of the sun. I rode alongside Princess Mary; returning home, we had to cross the Podkumok at a ford. The shallowest of mountain streams is dangerous, particularly because their beds are utterly kaleidoscopic: every day the pressure of the waves changes them; where yesterday there was a stone, today there's a hole. I took the Princess' horse by the bridle and led it down into the water, which came no higher than its knees; we gradually began to move diagonally against the current. It's well known that when crossing fast streams you ought not to look at the water, for your head will immediately start to spin. I forgot to tell Princess Mary about this beforehand.

We were already in midstream, in the very rapids, when she suddenly lurched in the saddle. 'I feel ill!' she said in a weak voice… I quickly leant towards her, wrapped my arm around her supple waist.

'Look up!' I whispered to her: 'It's all right, just don't be frightened; I'm with you.'

She recovered; she tried to free herself from my arm, but I further tightened my hold on her delicate, soft body: my cheek was almost touching her cheek; I could feel its fiery heat.

'What are you doing to me?… My God!…'

I paid no attention to her trembling and confusion, and my lips touched her delicate little cheek; she gave a start, but said nothing; we were bringing up the rear: nobody saw. When we climbed out onto the bank, everyone set off at a trot. The Princess held her horse back; I remained beside her; it was clear that my silence was troubling her, but I swore not to utter a word – out of curiosity. I wanted to see how she'd extricate herself from this difficult situation.

'Either you despise me, or you love me very much!' she finally said in a voice that had tears in it. 'Perhaps you want to mock me, stir up my soul and then leave me… That would be so vile, so base, that the supposition alone… Oh no! Isn't it true,' she added in a voice of tender trust, 'isn't it true that there's nothing about me that might preclude respect? Your presumptuous action… I must, I must forgive you it, because I allowed it… Answer me, speak, will you, I want to hear your voice!…' In the final words there was such feminine impatience that I gave an involuntary smile; fortunately, it was beginning to get dark… I made no reply.

'You remain silent?' she continued. 'Perhaps you want me to tell you that I love you first?'

I was silent…

'Is that what you want?' she continued, turning to me abruptly… In the resolution of her gaze and voice there was something terrible…

'What for?' I replied with a shrug.

She struck her horse with her whip and set off at top speed along the narrow, dangerous road; it happened so quickly that I was scarcely able to catch up with her, and only did so when she had already joined the rest of the party. Right up to her house she was talking and laughing constantly. In her movements there was something feverish; not once did she glance at me. Everyone noticed this extraordinary gaiety. And Princess Ligovskaya inwardly rejoiced, looking at her daughter; but the daughter's simply having a nervous attack: she'll spend a sleepless night crying. This thought gives me unbounded pleasure: there are moments when I understand the Vampyre[54]… And yet I'm still reputed to be a good fellow and I do strive for that designation!

Dismounting from their horses, the ladies went upstairs to the Princess'; I was agitated, and I galloped into the mountains to dispel the thoughts crowding in my head. The dewy evening was intoxicatingly cool. The moon was rising from behind the dark summits. Each stride of my unshod horse rang out dully in the silence of the gorges; I let my mount drink at a waterfall, greedily inhaled the fresh air of the southern night a couple of times, and set off on the journey back. I rode through the suburb. The lights were beginning to go out in the windows; the sentries on the rampart of the fort and the Cossacks in the surrounding pickets exchanged long drawn-out calls…

In one of the houses in the suburb, built on the edge of a ravine, I noticed an exceptional amount of light; from time to time the sound of discordant voices and cries rang out, betraying the carousing of military men. I dismounted and stole up to the window; a shutter that had been left slightly ajar allowed me to see the carousers and listen to their words to the full. They were talking about me.

The captain of dragoons, flushed with wine, banged his fist on the table, demanding attention.

'Gentlemen!' he said, 'It's quite unheard of. Pechorin must be taught a lesson! These upstarts from St Petersburg always get above themselves until you give them a bloody nose! He thinks he's the only one who's lived in society because he always wears clean gloves and polished boots.'

'And what an arrogant smile! Yet I'm sure at the same time he's a coward – yes, a coward!'

'I think so too,' said Grushnitsky. 'He likes laughing things off. I once came out with such things to him that another man would have hacked me to pieces on the spot, but Pechorin turned everything into a joke. It stands to reason, I didn't challenge him, because that was his business; and I didn't want to get involved either…'

'Grushnitsky's angry with him because he's taken the Princess away from him,' said somebody.

'Now see what they've got into their heads! It's true, I did chase after the Princess a bit, but I soon backed off, because I don't want to get married, and it's against my principles to compromise a girl.'

'I can absolutely assure you, he's the greatest of cowards – Pechorin, that is, not Grushnitsky – oh, Grushnitsky's a fine chap, and my true friend, what's more!' the captain of dragoons spoke again. 'Gentlemen! No one here's defending him? No one? So much the better! Do you want to test his courage? That'll keep us amused…'

'We do; only how?'

'Well listen, then: Grushnitsky's especially angry with him – he gets the leading role! He'll find fault with some nonsense or other and challenge Pechorin to a duel… Hang on, this is where the catch is… He'll challenge him to a duel – fine! All of it – the challenge, the preparations, the conditions – will be as solemn and frightful as possible; I take that upon myself; I'll be your second, my poor friend! Fine! Only this is where the trick comes: we won't put balls in the pistols. I'll be answerable to you myself, Pechorin'll chicken out – I'll have them six paces apart, damn it! Are you agreed, gentlemen?'

'Brilliant idea, we're agreed! Why ever not?' rang out on all sides.

'And you, Grushnitsky?'

Trembling, I awaited Grushnitsky's reply. I was possessed by cold fury at the thought that, had it not been for chance, I might have made myself a laughing stock for these fools. If Grushnitsky had refused to agree, I'd have thrown my arms around his neck. But after some silence he rose from his seat, reached his hand out to the captain, and said very pompously: 'All right, I agree.'

It's hard to describe the delight of the entire worthy crew.

I returned home, disturbed by two different feelings. The first was sadness. Why do they all hate me? I thought. Why? Have I offended anyone? No. Surely I don't number among the ranks of those whose appearance alone is enough to generate ill will? And I could feel that, little by little, venomous fury was filling my soul. 'Be careful, Mr Grushnitsky!' I said, pacing back and forth about the room. 'You don't joke like that with me. You may pay dearly for the approval of your stupid comrades. I'm not your plaything!'

I was awake all night. By morning I was as yellow as a Seville orange.

In the morning I met Princess Mary at the well.

'Are you ill?' she said, looking at me intently.

'I had a sleepless night.'

'I did too… I blamed you… perhaps wrongly? But explain yourself, I can forgive you everything…'

'Everything?…'

'Everything… only tell the truth… only quickly… You see, I've done a lot of thinking, trying to explain, to justify your behaviour;

perhaps you're afraid of my family creating obstacles… but that's nothing: when they get to know…' – her voice began to quaver – 'I'll persuade them. Or your own situation… but you should know I can make any sacrifice for the man I love… Oh, answer quickly – have pity… You don't despise me, do you?'

She seized me by the hand.

Princess Ligovskaya was walking ahead of us with Vera's husband and saw nothing; but we could be seen by patients out strolling – the most inquisitive gossips of them all – and I quickly freed my hand from her passionate grip.

'I'll tell you the whole truth,' I replied to the Princess: 'I won't try to justify myself, nor explain my actions. I don't love you.'

Her lips paled a little…

'Leave me,' she said, scarcely intelligibly.

I shrugged, turned around and walked away.

14TH JUNE

I despise myself sometimes… isn't that why I despise others too?… I've become incapable of noble impulses; I'm afraid of seeming ridiculous to myself. In my place another man would have offered the Princess *son cœur et sa fortune*[55]; but the word *marry* has some magical power over me: however passionately I love a woman, if she lets me so much as feel that I ought to marry her – goodbye to love! My heart is turned to stone, and nothing will warm it up again. I'm prepared for any sacrifice except that one; I'll stake my life, even my honour on a card twenty times… but I won't sell my freedom. Why do I prize it so? What does it hold for me?… What am I preparing myself for? What do I expect from the future?… Truly, absolutely nothing. It's a sort of innate terror, inexpressible foreboding… After all, there are people who have an unaccountable fear of spiders, cockroaches, mice… Should I admit it?… When I was still a child, an old woman told my fortune for my mother; she predicted my *death on account of a malevolent wife*; this affected me deeply at the time: in my soul was born an insuperable aversion to marriage… At the same time, something tells me her prediction will come true; at least I'll try to stop it coming true for as long as possible.

The conjuror 'Apfelbaum' arrived here yesterday. On the doors of the restaurant appeared a lengthy announcement, notifying the most esteemed public that the aforesaid amazing conjuror, acrobat, chemist and optician would have the honour of giving a magnificent performance on today's date at eight o'clock in the evening in the hall of the Nobles' Assembly Rooms (in other words – in the restaurant); tickets at two roubles fifty kopeks each.

Everyone means to go and see the amazing conjuror; even Princess Ligovskaya has got herself a ticket, despite the fact that her daughter is ill.

After lunch today I was walking past Vera's windows; she was sitting alone on the balcony; a note fell at my feet:

Come to me, using the main staircase, after nine o'clock this evening; my husband has left for Pyatigorsk and will return only tomorrow morning. My menservants and maids will be out of the house: I have given them all tickets, and the Princess' servants too. I am expecting you; come without fail.

'Aha!' I thought: 'at long last it's turned out the way I wanted.'

At eight o'clock I went to see the conjuror. The audience had assembled by the time nine approached; the performance began. In the rows of chairs at the back I recognised Vera's and the Princess' menservants and maids. Absolutely everyone was there. Grushnitsky sat in the front row with his lorgnette. The conjuror turned to him each time he needed a handkerchief, a watch, a ring and so on.

Grushnitsky hasn't been bowing to me for some time now, but today he looked at me a couple of times quite impertinently. He'll be reminded of it all when we come to settle our accounts.

Towards ten I got up and left.

It was dark outside, pitch black. Heavy, cold clouds lay on the summits of the surrounding mountains: only occasionally did the dying wind set the tops of the poplars that surrounded the restaurant rustling; people were crowding around the latter's windows. I went down the hill and, turning into the gates, I increased my pace. Suddenly it seemed to me that someone was following me. I stopped and looked around. Nothing could be made out in the darkness; however, out of caution I went all the way round the house, as if taking a stroll. While walking past Princess Mary's windows, I heard steps behind me once again, and a man wrapped up in a greatcoat ran past me. This alarmed me; however, I stole up to the porch and hurriedly ran up the dark stairs. A door opened; a little hand seized my hand…

'No one saw you?' said Vera in a whisper, nestling up against me.

'No one!'

'Now do you believe I love you? Oh, for a long time I wavered, for a long time I agonised… but you can do anything you like with me.'

Her heart was beating hard, her hands were cold as ice. There began reproaches, jealousy, complaints, she demanded I confess everything to her, saying she would bear my infidelity submissively because all she wanted was my happiness. I didn't entirely believe it, but soothed her with vows, promises and so on.

'So you're not going to marry Mary? You don't love her?… Yet she thinks… you know, she's madly in love with you, the poor thing!…'

At about two o'clock in the morning I opened a window and, after tying two shawls together, let myself down from an upper balcony onto a lower one while holding onto a column. A light was still burning in the Princess' room. Something pushed me towards that window. The curtain wasn't fully drawn, and I was able to cast an inquisitive glance into the room's interior. Mary was sitting on her bed with her arms crossed on her knees; her thick hair was gathered under a nightcap trimmed with lace; a large crimson shawl covered her little white shoulders, her small feet were hidden in vivid Persian slippers. She sat motionless, with her head lowered onto her breast; on a table in front of her was an open book, but her eyes, motionless and full of inexpressible sadness, seemed to have been skimming over one and the same page for the hundredth time, while her thoughts were far away…

At that moment somebody stirred behind a bush. I jumped down from the balcony onto the turf. An unseen hand grabbed me by the shoulder. 'Aha!' said a coarse voice: 'Got you!… I'll teach you to go calling on princesses in the night!…'

'Keep a tight hold on him!' shouted someone else who'd leapt out from around the corner.

It was Grushnitsky and the captain of dragoons.

I struck the latter on the head with my fist, knocked him down and rushed into the bushes. I knew all the paths in the garden that covered the slope opposite our houses.

'Thieves! Help!…' they cried; a gunshot rang out; a smoking wad fell almost at my feet.

A minute later I was already in my room, I undressed and got into bed. Scarcely had my manservant locked the door than Grushnitsky and the captain began knocking for me.

'Pechorin! Are you asleep? Are you there?…' cried the captain.

'I'm asleep,' I replied angrily.

'Get up! Thieves… Circassians…'

'I've got a blocked nose,' I replied: 'I'm afraid of catching a cold.'

They went away. I made a mistake responding to them; they'd have spent another hour or so searching for me in the garden. In the meantime a terrible alarm had gone up. A Cossack galloped up from the fort. Everything was set in motion; they started looking for Circassians in every bush – and, it goes without saying, found nothing. But many people probably remained firmly convinced that if the garrison had shown more courage and urgency then at least a couple of dozen marauders would have fallen where they stood.

16TH JUNE

At the well this morning there was talk of nothing but the Circassians' attack during the night. After drinking the requisite number of glasses of Narzan and walking up and down the long lime walk ten times or so, I met Vera's husband, who had only just arrived from Pyatigorsk. He took me by the arm, and we went to the restaurant for lunch; he was dreadfully worried about his wife. 'What a fright she had last night!' he said: 'I mean, didn't it just have to happen at the very time I was away?' We settled down to have lunch beside the door leading into the corner room where there were about ten young men, among whom was Grushnitsky too. For a second time fate provided me with an opportunity to eavesdrop on a conversation that was to decide his lot. He didn't see me, and consequently I couldn't suspect any intent; but that only increased his guilt in my eyes.

'Is it possible that it really was Circassians?' said someone. 'Did anybody see them?'

'I'll tell you the whole story,' replied Grushnitsky, 'only please don't give me away. This is how it was: yesterday a certain person, whose name I won't give you, comes to me and tells me that after nine o'clock in the evening he saw somebody stealing into the Ligovskayas' house. You should note that Princess Ligovskaya was here, while Princess Mary was at home. So he and I set out to lie in wait for the lucky fellow beneath the windows.'

I confess I had a fright, although my companion was very busy with his lunch: he could have heard things rather unpleasant for him, supposing that Grushnitsky had guessed the truth; but, blinded by jealousy, he didn't even suspect it.

'So you see,' continued Grushnitsky, 'we set off, taking with us a gun, loaded with a blank cartridge, just, you know, to frighten. We waited in the garden till two o'clock. Finally – God only knows where he appeared from, only not out of the window, because it didn't open, so he must have come out through the glass door that's behind the column – finally, I say, we see someone coming down from the balcony... What about that Princess, eh? Well, I've got to give it to them, Moscow girls! What on earth can you rely on after this? We tried to grab him, only he broke free and raced like a hare into the bushes; at that point I fired after him.'

A murmur of mistrust rang out around Grushnitsky.

'Don't you believe it?' he continued; 'I give you my word of honour as a gentleman that all this is the absolute truth, and as proof, if you like, I'll give you the man's name.'

'Tell us, tell us, whoever is it?' rang out on all sides.

'Pechorin,' replied Grushnitsky.

At that moment he raised his eyes – I was standing in the doorway opposite him; he turned terribly red. I went up to him and said, slowly and distinctly:

'I'm very sorry I came in after you'd already given your word of honour in confirmation of the most disgusting slander. My presence would have saved you from a further vile act.'

Grushnitsky leapt up from his seat, meaning to get heated.

'I request,' I continued in the same tone: 'I request that you retract your words immediately; you know very well that it's a fabrication. I don't think a woman's indifference to your brilliant qualities deserves such terrible vengeance. Have a good think: by maintaining your opinion, you forfeit the right to be called a gentleman and you put your life at risk.'

Grushnitsky stood before me with downcast eyes, greatly agitated. But the struggle of conscience with vanity was short-lived. The captain of dragoons, who was sitting beside him, nudged him with his elbow; he gave a start and replied to me quickly, without raising his eyes:

'My dear sir, when I say something, then that's what I think, and I'm prepared to repeat it... I'm not afraid of your threats and I'm prepared to do anything.'

'You've already proved the latter point,' I answered him coldly and, taking the captain of dragoons by the arm, left the room.

'What do you want?' asked the captain.

'You're a close acquaintance of Grushnitsky's and I suppose you'll act as his second?'

The captain gave a very pompous bow.

'Your guess is right,' he replied: 'I'm obliged, even, to act as his second, because the aspersion cast at him applies to me too: I was with him last night,' he added, straightening his rather stooping figure.

'Ah, so it was you I hit so clumsily on the head?'

He turned yellow, then blue; his face was a picture of concealed malice.

'I shall have the honour to send my second to you this very day,' I added, taking my leave with a very polite bow and pretending to pay no attention to his fury.

On the porch of the restaurant I met Vera's husband. He appeared to have been waiting for me.

He seized my hand with an emotion that resembled rapture.

'You noble young man!' he said, with tears in his eyes. 'I heard it all. What an ungrateful swine!... Receive them in a respectable house after this! Thank God I have no daughters! But you'll have your reward from the one you're risking your life for. Be assured of my discretion for the time being,' he continued. 'I've been young myself and served in the military; I know one shouldn't get involved in these affairs. Farewell.'

The poor man! He's glad he has no daughters...

I went straight to Werner's, found him in and told him everything – my relations with Vera and Princess Mary and the conversation I'd overheard, from which I'd learnt of these gentlemen's intention to make a fool of me by compelling me to fight a duel with blank cartridges. But now the matter was going beyond the bounds of a joke: they probably hadn't expected such a denouement.

The doctor agreed to be my second; I gave him a number of instructions regarding the conditions of the duel; he was to insist on the matter being settled as secretly as possible, because although I'm prepared to expose myself to death whenever you like, I'm not at all well disposed to ruining my future for good in this world.

After that I went home. An hour later the doctor returned from his expedition.

'There's a conspiracy against you for sure,' he said. 'At Grushnitsky's I found the captain of dragoons and one other gentleman whose name I don't remember. I stopped for a minute in the hallway to take off my galoshes. There was a terrible noise and argument going on there... "I won't agree, not for anything!" Grushnitsky said. "He insulted me in public; it was completely different then..." – "What is it to you?" answered the captain: "I take it all upon myself. I've been a second at five duels, and I know how to arrange it. I've thought of everything. Only please, don't stop me. Giving a bit of a scare does no harm. And why expose yourself to danger if it can be avoided?..." At that moment I went in. They suddenly fell silent. Our negotiations went on for quite a while; in the end this is how we decided the matter: about five kilometres from here there's an out of-the-way gorge; they'll go there tomorrow at four in the morning, and we'll ride out half an hour after them; you'll shoot at six paces – Grushnitsky himself demanded it. The one who's killed is put down to Circassians. Now, these are the suspicions I have: they, that is the seconds probably, have altered their former plan somewhat, and want to load only Grushnitsky's pistol with a ball. That's a little reminiscent of murder, but in time of war, and especially in an Asiatic war, wiles are permitted; only Grushnitsky seems a little nobler than his comrades. What do you think? Ought we to show them that we've guessed?'

'Not for anything on earth, Doctor! Don't worry: I won't give in to them.'

'What do you mean to do, then?'

'That's my secret.'

'Watch you don't get caught out… after all, at six paces!'

'Doctor, I'll expect you tomorrow at four a.m.; the horses will be ready… Farewell.'

I stayed at home until the evening, locked in my room. A footman came to invite me to Princess Ligovskaya's – I ordered him to say I was ill.

Two o'clock in the morning… I can't sleep… although I ought to get to sleep so my hand doesn't shake tomorrow. Still, at six paces it's hard to miss. Ah, Mr Grushnitsky! Your hoax won't come off for you… we're going to swap roles: now I shall have to search your pale face for signs of secret fear. Why did you yourself designate those fateful six paces? You think I'll make myself a target for you without an argument… but we're going to cast lots!… and then… then… what if his good fortune has the edge? What if my star finally betrays me?… And it'd be no wonder: it's served my whims faithfully for so long; and there's no more constancy in the heavens than there is on earth.

Well, then? If I'm to die, so be it! No great loss to the world; and I'm already pretty bored myself. I'm like a man yawning at a ball, who doesn't go off to bed simply because his carriage hasn't yet come. But when the carriage is ready… farewell!…

I run through all my past life in my memory and involuntarily wonder: what have I lived for? For what purpose was I born?… Yet it probably did exist, and I probably had a lofty designation, because in my soul I sense unbounded powers… But I failed to divine that designation and fell for the enticements of empty and thankless passions; I emerged from their crucible hard and cold as iron, but I'd lost for ever the ardour of noble aspirations – life's finest flower. And how many times already since then have I played the role of an axe in the hands of fate! Like an instrument of execution I've fallen on the heads of doomed victims, often without malice, always without regret... My love has brought happiness to no one, because I've sacrificed nothing for those I've loved: I've loved for myself, for my own pleasure; I've only satisfied the strange demand of my heart, greedily devouring their feelings, their tenderness, their joys and sufferings – and I could never get my fill. Thus a man racked by hunger falls asleep in exhaustion and sees before him sumptuous foods and sparkling wines; in delight he gobbles up the ethereal fruits of his imagination and he seems to feel better; but no sooner has he woken up – the dream vanishes... there remains double the hunger and despair!

And maybe tomorrow I shall die!... And not a single creature will be left on earth that will have understood me fully. Some think me worse, others better than I really am... Some will say: he was a good fellow; others – a swine. Both the one and the other will be wrong. Is living worth the effort after this? But you keep on living – out of curiosity: you expect something new... It's ridiculous and annoying!

* * * * *

It's already a month and a half now that I've been at the fort of N***; Maxim Maximych has gone off hunting... I'm alone; I'm sitting by the window; grey clouds have covered the mountains down to their feet; the sun through the mist seems like a yellow blot. It's cold; the wind is blowing and rocking the shutters... I'm bored!... I'll continue with my journal, interrupted by so many strange events.

I'm reading over the last page: it's ridiculous! I thought of dying; that was impossible: I hadn't yet drained the cup of suffering, and now I sense that I've a long time yet to live.

How clearly and sharply has all the past been cast in my memory! Not a single feature, not a single tone has been erased by time!

I remember that during the night preceding the duel I didn't sleep for a minute. I couldn't write for long: a secret disquiet took hold of me. For about an hour I paced about the room; then I sat down and opened the Walter Scott novel that lay on my desk: it was *Old Mortality*; I found reading an effort at first, then I forgot myself, carried away by the magical invention... The Scottish bard is surely repaid in the other world for every comforting moment his book brings...

Finally the day dawned. My nerves were calmed. I looked at myself in the mirror; a dull pallor covered my face, which retained the traces of agonising insomnia; but the eyes, though ringed with brown shadows, shone proudly and implacably. I was pleased with myself.

After ordering the horses to be saddled, I dressed and ran down to the bathing place. Immersing myself in the cold, seething Narzan, I felt my bodily and spiritual powers returning. I emerged from the bathhouse fresh and cheerful, as if getting ready for a ball. Say after that that the spirit doesn't depend on the body!...

Returning home, I found the doctor there. He was wearing grey riding breeches, a kaftan and a Circassian hat. I roared with laughter when I saw that little figure underneath a huge, shaggy hat: his face isn't at all belligerent, and on this occasion it was even longer than normal.

'Why are you so sad, Doctor?' I said to him. 'Haven't you seen people off to the other world a hundred times with the greatest indifference? Imagine I've got bilious fever; I may recover, I may die too; both the one and the other are in the order of things; try and look upon me as a patient in the grip of an illness as yet unknown to you – and then your curiosity will be aroused to the highest degree; now you can make a number of important physiological observations about me... Isn't expectation of a violent death a genuine illness in itself?'

The doctor was struck by this idea and cheered up.

We mounted our horses; Werner took hold of the reins with both hands and we set off – in a moment we'd galloped past the fort, through the suburb and entered the gorge, along which wound a road half overgrown with tall grass and continually intersected by a noisy stream which had to be forded, to the great despair of the doctor, because his horse came to a halt in the water every time.

I can't remember a morning more blue and fresh! The sun had barely appeared from behind the green hilltops, and the intermingling of the first warmth of its rays with the dying cool of the night laid a sweet sort of languor on all one's senses; the joyous ray of the young day had not yet penetrated the gorge; it gilded only the tops of the crags that hung over us on both sides; the dense foliage of the bushes that grew in their deep crevices showered us with silver rain at the least breath of wind. I remember – on that morning, more than ever before,

I loved nature. How inquisitively I peered at every dewdrop trembling on a broad vine leaf and reflecting millions of iridescent rays! How greedily my gaze tried to penetrate the smoky distance! There the road became ever narrower, the crags bluer and more terrifying, and finally they seemed to merge in an impenetrable wall. We rode in silence.

'Have you written your will?' asked Werner suddenly.

'No.'

'But what if you're killed?…'

'Heirs'll turn up by themselves.'

'Have you really no friends you'd like to send a last farewell to?…'

I shook my head.

'Is there really no woman on earth you'd like to leave something to as a memento?…'

'Doctor,' I answered him, 'do you want me to bare my soul to you?… You see, I'm past the age when people die uttering the name of their beloved and bequeathing to their friend a little tuft of greased or ungreased hair. When thinking of imminent and possible death, I think of myself alone: some don't even do that. Friends who'll forget me tomorrow or, worse, hold me to account for God knows what cock-and-bull stories; women who, while embracing another man, will laugh about me so as not to arouse in him any jealousy of the deceased – to hell with them! From life's storm I've carried out just a few ideas – and not a single feeling. I've been living for a long time now not by the heart, but by the head. I weigh up and analyse my own passions and actions with stern curiosity, but without sympathy. There are two men inside me: one lives in the full sense of the word, the other ponders and judges him; in an hour's time the first will perhaps say farewell to you and the world for good, while the second… the second?… Look, Doctor: can you see three black figures on the cliff to the right? They would seem to be our adversaries?…'

We broke into a trot.

Three horses were tethered in the bushes at the foot of the cliff; we tethered ours there too, and we ourselves clambered up a narrow path to a little ledge where Grushnitsky was awaiting us with the captain of dragoons and his other second who was called Ivan Ignatyevich; I never heard his surname.

'We've already been waiting for you a long time,' said the captain of dragoons, with an ironic smile.

I took out my watch and showed him.

He apologised, saying that his watch was fast.

A difficult silence lasted for several moments; finally the doctor broke it by turning to Grushnitsky:

'It seems to me,' he said, 'that as you've both shown your readiness to fight and thus paid your due to the conventions of honour, you could, gentlemen, talk things over and conclude this affair amicably.'

'I'm prepared to,' I said.

The captain winked at Grushnitsky, and the latter, thinking I was getting cold feet, adopted a proud air, although until this moment a dull pallor had covered his cheeks. For the first time since we'd arrived he raised his eyes to look at me; but in his gaze there was a sort of anxiety that disclosed an inner struggle.

'Explain your conditions,' he said, 'and anything that I can do for you, rest assured…'

'Here are my conditions: this very day you'll publicly retract your slander and beg my pardon…'

'My dear sir, I'm amazed you dare propose such things to me…'

'But what else could I have proposed to you other than that?…'

'We're going to have the duel.'

I shrugged.

'As you wish; only think about the fact that one of us will be killed for sure.'

'I want it to be you…'

'But I'm so sure of the reverse…'

He became embarrassed, blushed, then gave a forced chuckle.

The captain took him by the arm and led him aside; they spent a long time whispering. I'd arrived in quite a peaceable frame of mind, but all this was beginning to infuriate me.

The doctor approached me.

'Listen,' he said, with obvious anxiety: 'you must have forgotten about their plot?… I don't know how to load a pistol, but in this case… You're a strange man! Tell them you know their intention and they won't dare… What is it you want? They'll shoot you down like a bird…'

'Please don't worry, Doctor, and just wait… I'll arrange everything in such a way that there'll be no advantage on their side. Let them whisper for a bit…'

'Gentlemen, this is getting boring!' I said to them loudly. 'If we're going to fight, then let's fight; you had the time to talk all you wanted yesterday…'

'We're ready,' replied the captain. 'Take your positions, gentlemen!… Doctor, be so good as to measure out six paces…'

'Take your positions!' repeated Ivan Ignatyevich in a squeaky voice.

'Allow me!' I said. 'One more condition: since we'll be fighting to the death, we're bound to do everything possible so that it remains a secret and our seconds aren't held responsible. Do you agree?…'

'We totally agree.'

'So this is what I've come up with. Do you see at the top of that steep cliff, on the right, the narrow little ledge? From there to the bottom will be about sixty metres, if not more; there are sharp rocks down below. Each of us will stand on the very edge of the ledge; that way even a slight wound will be fatal: that ought to be in accordance with your wish, because you designated six paces yourself. Anyone who's wounded will be sure to fall and will be smashed to smithereens; the doctor will take out the ball, and then it'll be very easy to explain this sudden death as an unfortunate leap. We'll draw lots to see who fires first. I declare to you in conclusion that otherwise I won't fight.'

'As you wish!' said the captain, after an expressive look at Grushnitsky, who nodded his consent. His face was continually changing. I'd put him in a difficult position. Duelling under normal conditions, he could have aimed at my leg, wounded me slightly and thus had his revenge without overburdening his conscience; but now he had to fire into the air, or become a murderer, or, finally, abandon his vile plan and expose himself to just the same danger as me. At that moment I wouldn't have wished to be in his place. He led the captain aside and started saying something to him very heatedly; his lips had gone blue, and I could see them trembling; but the captain turned away from him with a contemptuous smile. 'You're a fool!' he said to Grushnitsky quite loudly. 'You don't understand a thing! Let's be off, then, gentlemen!'

A narrow path led up the steep slope between bushes; the debris of the cliffs formed the unsteady steps of this natural staircase; clutching at the bushes, we started scrambling up. Grushnitsky led the way, followed by his seconds, and then by the doctor and me.

'I'm amazed at you,' said the doctor, squeezing my arm tight. 'Let me feel your pulse!... Oho! Feverish!... But nothing's noticeable in the face... Only your eyes are shining brighter than normal.'

Suddenly some small stones rolled noisily under our feet. What was it? Grushnitsky had stumbled; the branch at which he'd clutched had broken, and he would have slid down on his back if his seconds hadn't held him up.

'Watch out!' I called to him. 'Don't fall down ahead of time; that's a bad omen. Remember Julius Caesar!⁵⁶'

So we clambered up onto the top of the overhanging cliff; the ledge was covered with fine sand, as though specially for a duel. Mountain peaks, disappearing in the golden mist of morning, crowded all around like an innumerable herd, and in the south rose the white hulk of Elbrus, concluding the chain of snowy peaks between which there already roamed some wispy clouds that had raced up from the east. I went over to the edge of the ledge and looked down, and my head almost started spinning: there down below it seemed as dark and cold as the tomb; the mossy teeth of the cliffs, cast down by thunderstorm and time, awaited their prey.

The ledge on which we were to fight formed an almost regular triangle. Six paces were measured out from the projecting corner, and it was decided that the one who had to face hostile fire first would stand on the very corner with his back to the abyss; if he weren't killed, then the adversaries would change places.

I'd made up my mind to present Grushnitsky with every advantage; I wanted to test him out; a spark of magnanimity might have awoken in his soul, and then everything would have been settled for the best; but vanity and weakness of character were to triumph... I wanted to give myself every right to have no mercy on him if fate were to spare me. Who hasn't agreed on such conditions with his conscience?

'Cast lots, Doctor!' said the captain.

The doctor took a silver coin from his pocket and held it up.

'Tails!' called Grushnitsky hastily, like a man who's suddenly been woken up with a friendly nudge.

'Heads!' said I.

The coin span up and fell with a ringing sound; everybody rushed towards it.

'You're fortunate,' I said to Grushnitsky: 'you're the first to fire! But remember that if you don't kill me, I won't miss – I give you my word of honour.'

He blushed; he was ashamed to kill an unarmed man; I gazed at him intently; for a minute or so it seemed to me he would throw himself at my feet, begging forgiveness; but how can you admit to such a base design?... One course remained to him – to fire into the air; I was certain he would fire into the air! One thing might prevent it: the idea that I'd demand a second duel.

'It's time!' the doctor whispered to me, tugging at my sleeve. 'If you don't tell them now that we know their intentions, then all is lost. Look, he's already loading... if you don't say something, then I'll –'

'Not for anything in the world, Doctor!' I replied, restraining him by the arm. 'You'll spoil everything; you gave me your word not to interfere... What's it to you? Perhaps I want to be killed...'

He looked at me in surprise.

'Oh! That's another matter!... Only don't complain about me in the other world...'

The captain, meanwhile, had loaded his pistols. He handed one to Grushnitsky, whispering something to him with a smile; the other to me.

I stood on the corner of the ledge, wedging my left leg firmly against a rock and leaning forwards a little, so as not to topple backwards in the event of a slight wound.

Grushnitsky stood opposite me and, when the signal was given, began to raise his pistol. His knees were trembling. He was aiming straight at my forehead...

An inexpressible fury started to boil up in my breast.

Suddenly he lowered the barrel of the pistol and, going white as a sheet, he turned to his second:

'I can't,' he said in a hollow voice.

'Coward!' replied the captain.

A shot rang out. The ball grazed my knee. I involuntarily took several steps forward to get away quickly from the edge.

'Well, Grushnitsky, old fellow, it's a shame you missed!' said the captain. 'It's your turn now, take your position! But give me a hug first; we shan't meet again!' They hugged one another; the captain could hardly stop himself laughing. 'Don't be afraid,' he added, glancing slyly at Grushnitsky, 'everything on earth is nonsense!... Creation's an aberration, fate's batty, and life's tatty!'

After this tragic phrase, spoken with decent pomposity, he withdrew to his position; Ivan Ignatyich also embraced Grushnitsky tearfully, and then the latter remained alone opposite me. I'm still trying to explain to myself what sort of emotion was then boiling in my breast: it was both the annoyance of injured vanity, and contempt, and also malice, born of the thought that this man gazing at me now with such certainty, with such calm impertinence, had two minutes before, without exposing himself to any danger, tried to kill me like a dog, for if wounded a little more seriously in the leg, I would have toppled from the cliff for certain.

I looked him intently in the face for several moments, trying to discern even a slight trace of repentance. But it seemed to me that he was holding back a smile.

'I advise you to pray to God before you die,' I then said to him.

'Have no more concern for my soul than you do for your own. I ask one thing of you: hurry up and fire.'

'And you don't withdraw your slander? You don't ask my forgiveness?... Have a good think: does your conscience not tell you anything?'

'Mr Pechorin!' cried the captain of dragoons: 'Allow me to point out you're not here to take confession... Let's hurry up and finish; suppose somebody comes riding through the gorge – and sees us.'

'Very well. Doctor, come over here.'

The doctor came over. The poor doctor! He was paler than Grushnitsky ten minutes before.

The next words I deliberately pronounced without haste, loudly and distinctly, as a death sentence is pronounced.

'Doctor, these gentlemen, probably being in a hurry, forgot to put a ball in my pistol: please load it anew – and properly!'

'It's not possible!' cried the captain. 'It's not possible! I loaded both pistols; it can only be that the ball's rolled out of yours... That's not my fault! But you don't have the right to reload... no right at all... it's completely against the rules; I won't allow it...'

'Very well!' I said to the captain. 'If that's the way it is, you and I will fight a duel under the same conditions...'

He stopped short.

Grushnitsky stood with his head down on his chest, embarrassed and gloomy.

'Leave them alone!' he finally said to the captain, who was trying to tear my pistol out of the doctor's hands... 'After all, you know for yourself they're right.'

The captain made various signs to him in vain – Grushnitsky didn't even want to look.

Meanwhile the doctor had loaded the pistol and handed it to me.

Seeing this, the captain spat and stamped his foot. 'You're a fool, old chap,' he said: 'a regular fool!... Once you'd put your trust in me, you should've done everything you were told... It serves you right! Get yourself killed like a fly...' He turned aside and, walking away, muttered: 'But all the same, it's completely against the rules.'

'Grushnitsky!' I said: 'There's still time; withdraw your slander and I'll forgive you everything. You didn't succeed in making a fool of me, and my vanity's satisfied; remember – we were once friends...'

His face flared up, his eyes flashed.

'Shoot!' he replied: 'I despise myself and I hate you. If you don't kill me, I'll knife you from around a corner in the night. There isn't room on earth for the two of us...'

I fired...

When the smoke cleared, Grushnitsky wasn't on the ledge. Only a slight column of dust was still swirling on the edge of the precipice.

Everyone cried out in unison.

'*Finita la commedia!*'[57] I said to the doctor.

He didn't reply, and turned away in horror.

I shrugged my shoulders and bowed to Grushnitsky's seconds.

Going down the path, I noticed Grushnitsky's bloodied corpse between the fissures of the cliffs. I involuntarily closed my eyes...

Untethering my horse, I set off for home at a walking pace. There was a stone in my heart. The sun seemed dim to me, its rays didn't warm me.

Before I reached the suburb I turned right along the gorge. The sight of a person would have been distressing for me: I wanted to be alone. Dropping the reins and with my head on my chest, I rode for a long time and finally found myself in a place completely unknown to me; I turned my mount back and began searching for the road; the sun was already setting when I approached Kislovodsk, exhausted on an exhausted horse.

My manservant told me that Werner had called, and he handed me two notes: one from him, the other... from Vera.

I opened the first; its content was as follows:

All's been arranged as well as possible: the body brought back disfigured, the ball removed from the chest. All are certain that the cause of his death was an accident; only the commandant, who's probably aware of your quarrel, shook his head, but said nothing. There's no evidence against you at all, and you can sleep easily... if you can... Farewell...

I couldn't bring myself to open the second note for a long time... What could she have written to me?... A heavy foreboding disturbed my soul.

Here it is, that letter, each word of which is indelibly engraved on my memory:

I am writing to you in the full certainty that we shall never see each other again. Several years ago, when parting from you, I thought the same; but Heaven was pleased to test me for a second time; I failed to withstand that test, my weak heart submitted anew to a familiar voice... you will not despise me for that, will you? This letter will be a farewell and a confession combined: I am bound to tell you everything that has mounted up in my heart in the time it has loved you. I will not think of blaming you – you have behaved with me as any other man would have done: you have loved me as your property, as a source of the alternating joys, alarms and sorrows without which life is dull and monotonous. I realised that from the start... But you were unhappy, and I sacrificed myself, hoping that some day you would appreciate my sacrifice, that some day you would understand my deep tenderness, independent of all conditions. A great deal of time has passed since then: I have penetrated into all the secrets of your soul... and become convinced that that was a vain hope. I was bitter! But my love has knitted with my soul: it has grown darker, but not gone out.

We are parting for good; you can be sure, however, that I shall never love another: my soul has exhausted all its treasures on you, its tears and hopes. A woman who has once loved you cannot look at other men without a certain scorn, not because you are better than them, oh no! But there is something particular in your nature, characteristic of you alone, something proud and mysterious; in your voice, whatever you might say, there is invincible power; no one knows how to wish so constantly to be loved; in no one is evil so attractive; no one's gaze promises so much bliss; no one knows how to exploit his advantages better, and no one can be so truly unhappy as you, because no one tries so hard to assure himself of the contrary.

Now I must explain to you the reason for my hasty departure; it will appear insignificant to you, because it concerns me alone.

This morning my husband came into my room and told me about your quarrel with Grushnitsky. My expression evidently changed greatly, because he looked me intently in the eye for a long time; I almost lost consciousness at the thought that you must fight a duel today and I am the cause of it; I thought I should go mad... But now that I can be rational, I am sure you will remain alive: it is impossible for you to die without me, impossible! My husband paced about the room for a long time; I do not know what he said to me, I do not remember what I answered him... I probably told him that I love you... I only remember that at the end of our conversation he insulted me with an awful word and left the room. I heard him order the carriage to be harnessed... It is three hours now that I have been sitting by the window and waiting for your return... But you are alive, you cannot die!... The carriage is almost ready... Farewell,

farewell... I am lost – but what does it matter?... If I could be
certain that you will always remember me – I do not even say love,
no, only remember... Farewell; someone is coming... I must hide the
letter...

You don't love Mary, do you? You're not going to marry her?
Listen, you must make this sacrifice for me: I've lost everything in
the world for you...

Like a madman I leapt out onto the porch, jumped onto my Circassian, who was being led round the courtyard, and set off at full pelt along the road to Pyatigorsk. I mercilessly drove my exhausted mount on, and he, wheezing and covered in lather, sped me along the stony road.

The sun had already hidden itself in a black cloud resting on the crest of the western mountains; the gorge had become dark and damp. The Podkumok scrambled across the rocks with a muffled and monotonous roaring. I galloped, choking with impatience. The thought of finding her no longer in Pyatigorsk struck at my heart like a hammer. For one minute, for one more minute to see her, to say goodbye, to squeeze her hand... I prayed, cursed, cried, laughed... no, nothing will express my disquiet, despair!... At the prospect of losing her for ever, Vera had become dearer to me than anything on earth – dearer than life, honour, happiness! God knows what strange, what crazy schemes swarmed in my head... And in the meantime I kept on galloping, mercilessly driving on. And then I began to notice that my mount was breathing more heavily; already he had stumbled a couple of times on level ground... There were five kilometres left to Essentuki – a Cossack village where I could change to another horse.

All would have been saved if my mount had had enough strength for another ten minutes. But suddenly, while climbing up out of a small gully as we emerged from the mountains, on a tight bend he crashed to the ground. I leapt off nimbly, tried to get him up, tugged at the rein – to no avail: a barely audible groan burst out through his clenched teeth; a few minutes later he was dead; I remained alone in the steppe, my last hope lost; I tried to continue on foot – my legs buckled; worn out by the alarms of the day and lack of sleep, I fell onto the wet grass and started crying like a child.

And for a long time I lay motionless and cried bitterly, without attempting to hold back the tears and the sobbing; I thought my breast would be torn apart; all my firmness, all my sangfroid vanished like smoke; my soul had lost its strength, my reason had fallen silent, and if anyone had seen me at that moment, they would have turned away in scorn.

When the night dew and the mountain breeze had refreshed my burning head, and my thoughts had returned to their normal order, I realised that chasing after lost happiness was useless and senseless. What more did I need? To see her? Why? Wasn't everything over between us? One bitter farewell kiss wouldn't enrich my memories, and after it we would only find it harder to part.

It's nice for me, however, to be able to cry! But perhaps jangled nerves, a night spent without sleep, two minutes facing the barrel of a pistol and an empty stomach were the cause of that.

All's for the best! This new suffering, speaking in the military style, created a fortunate diversion in me. Crying's healthy, and then if I'd not gone for a ride on horseback and not been forced to walk fifteen kilometres back again, I'd probably not have slept a wink that night either.

I got back to Kislovodsk at five o'clock in the morning, dropped onto my bed and fell into a sleep like Napoleon's after the Battle of Waterloo.

When I woke up, it was already dark outside. I sat down by the open window, unbuttoned my jacket – and the mountain breeze refreshed my breast, which had not yet been calmed by the heavy sleep of tiredness. In the distance beyond the river, through the tops of the dense limes overhanging it, lights could be glimpsed in the buildings of the fort and the suburb. All was quiet in our yard, Princess Ligovskaya's house was in darkness.

The doctor came up: there was a frown on his forehead; contrary to his custom, he didn't extend his hand to me.

'Where have you come from, Doctor?'

'From Princess Ligovskaya's; her daughter's ill – enervation… But that's not the point, the thing is this: the authorities guess what's happened, and although nothing can be positively proved, I nonetheless advise you to be a bit careful. Princess Ligovskaya was telling me today that she knows you fought a duel on behalf of her daughter. That little old man told her everything... what's his name? He witnessed your clash with Grushnitsky in the restaurant. I came to warn you. Farewell. We may not see one another again: they'll send you away somewhere.'

He paused on the threshold: he wanted to shake my hand... and if I'd shown him the slightest desire for it, he'd have flung his arms around my neck; but I remained as cold as stone – and he left.

There's people for you! They're all like that: they know in advance all the bad sides of an action, they help, give advice, even give it their approval, seeing the impossibility of any other way – and then they wash their hands and turn away indignantly from the man who's had the courage to take the whole weight of responsibility upon himself. They're all like that, even the kindest, the cleverest!...

The next morning, after receiving orders from senior officers to leave for the fort of N***, I dropped in on Princess Ligovskaya to say goodbye.

She was surprised when, to her question whether I had anything especially important to say to her, I replied that I wished her happiness and so on.

'Well, I need to have a very serious talk with you.'

I sat down in silence.

It was clear she didn't know where to begin; her face turned purple, her pudgy fingers tapped on the table; finally she began in a broken voice like this:

'Listen, Monsieur Pechorin; I think you're a noble man.'

I bowed.

'I'm sure of it, even,' she continued, 'although your behaviour is somewhat dubious; but you may have reasons of which I'm unaware, and it's those you must now confide to me. You've defended my daughter from slander, fought a duel on her behalf – consequently, risked your life... Don't reply, I know you won't admit it, because Grushnitsky's dead.' (She crossed herself.) 'God will forgive him, and – I hope – you too!... That doesn't concern me... I don't dare to condemn you, because my daughter, albeit innocently, was the cause of it. She's told me everything... I think, everything: you declared your

135

love to her… she admitted her own to you.' (Here the Princess sighed heavily.) 'But she's ill, and I'm sure it's not a simple illness! A secret sorrow is killing her; she doesn't admit it, but I'm sure you're the cause of it… Listen: perhaps you think I'm looking for rank, enormous wealth – be reassured: I want only my daughter's happiness. Your present position is unenviable, but it may improve: you're a man of means; my daughter loves you, she's been raised in such a way that she will make her husband happy. I'm rich, she's my only child… Speak, what holds you back?… You see, I shouldn't have said all this to you, but I'm counting on your heart, on your honour; remember, I have one daughter… one…'

She started to cry.

'Princess,' I said: 'I can't answer you; allow me to speak to your daughter in private…'

'Never!' she exclaimed, rising from her chair in great agitation.

'As you wish,' I replied, preparing to leave.

She became pensive, gestured to me that I should wait, and left the room.

About five minutes passed; my heart was beating hard, but my thoughts were calm, my head cool; however much I searched in my breast for even one spark of love for sweet Mary, my efforts were in vain.

Then the doors opened, and in she came. God! How she'd changed since I'd seen her last – and had it been long?

On reaching the middle of the room she staggered; I leapt up, gave her my arm and led her to a chair.

I stood facing her. We were silent for a long time; her large eyes, filled with inexpressible sadness, seemed to be searching in mine for something resembling hope; her pale lips tried in vain to smile; her delicate hands, folded on her knees, were so thin and transparent that I began to feel sorry for her.

'Princess,' I said: 'do you know I was mocking you? You ought to despise me.'

An unhealthy flush appeared on her cheeks.

I continued: 'Therefore, you cannot love me…'

She turned away, leant on a table, put her hands over her eyes, and it appeared to me that tears flashed in them.

'My God!' she uttered, scarcely intelligibly.

This was becoming unbearable: another minute and I'd have fallen at her feet.

'So you can see for yourself,' I said, in as firm a voice as I could and with a forced grin: 'you can see for yourself that I can't marry you. If you even wanted it now, you'd soon repent of it. My conversation with your mother forced me to have things out with you so frankly and so brutally; I hope she's deluded: you can easily disabuse her. You see, in your eyes I'm playing the most pitiful and disgusting role, and I even admit it; that's all I can do for you. Whatever bad opinion you might have of me, I submit to it... Do you see, I'm base before you... Even if you did love me, from this moment on you despise me, don't you?...'

She turned towards me, pale as marble, only her eyes were sparkling wonderfully.

'I hate you...' she said.

I thanked her, bowed respectfully and left.

An hour later a courier's troika was speeding me out of Kislovodsk. A few kilometres from Essentuki I recognised the corpse of my dashing mount close by the road; the saddle had been removed – probably by a passing Cossack – and on its back instead of the saddle sat two ravens. I sighed and turned away...

And now, here in this boring fort, I often wonder, as I run over the past in my mind, why I didn't want to step onto that path, opened up to me by fate, where quiet joys and spiritual tranquillity awaited me?... No, I wouldn't have got on with such a lot! I'm like a sailor, born and raised on the deck of a pirate brig: his soul has grown accustomed to storms and battles, and, cast up on the shore, he pines and languishes, no matter how the shady grove entices him, no matter how the peaceful sun shines for him; he wanders all day long over the seaside sand, listens intently to the monotonous murmur of the oncoming waves and peers closely into the misty distance, in case there – on the pale line dividing the blue deep from the grey clouds – the sail he longs for might be glimpsed, at first like the wing of a seagull, but little by little becoming distinct from the foam on the rocks, and running smoothly up towards the deserted haven...

3

The Fatalist

I once happened to live for two weeks in a Cossack village on the left flank; an infantry battalion was stationed there too; the officers gathered in each other's billets by turns and in the evenings played cards.

One day, bored of boston and with the cards thrown under the table, we sat up at Major S***'s for a very long time; the conversation, contrary to the norm, was absorbing. We were discussing the fact that the Muslim belief in a man's fate being written in the heavens finds many adherents among us Christians too; everyone related various unusual instances *pro* or *contra*.

'All this proves nothing, gentlemen,' said the old major: 'after all, none of you was a witness to these strange incidents with which you're corroborating your opinions?'

'None, of course,' said many: 'but we've heard from reliable people…'

'This is all nonsense,' said someone. 'Where are these reliable people who've seen the list on which the hour of our death is fixed?… And if there really is predestination, then why ever are we given free will, reason? Why must we account for our actions?'

At this point an officer who had been sitting in the corner of the room got up and, slowly approaching the table, cast a calm and triumphant gaze around at everyone. He was a Serb by birth, as was evident from his name.

Lieutenant Vulic's appearance corresponded fully with his character. Tall stature and a swarthy complexion, black hair, piercing black eyes, a large but regular nose – a characteristic of his nation – a sad and cold smile that forever flitted over his lips – it was as if it had all been coordinated to give him the look of a special being, incapable of sharing his thoughts and passions with those fate had given him as comrades.

He was courageous, spoke little, but sharply; confided his spiritual and family secrets to no one; drank almost no wine at all, never ran after the young Cossack girls – whose charm is hard to comprehend unless you have seen them. It was said, however, that the wife of the colonel was not indifferent to his expressive eyes; but he grew really angry when anyone alluded to this.

There was only one passion that he did not hide – a passion for gambling. At the green table he would forget everything, and normally lost; but constant failures only aggravated his obstinacy. The story went that once in the night-time during an expedition, he was the banker in a game of faro being played on his pillow; he was having terribly good luck. Suddenly shots rang out, the alarm was sounded, everybody leapt up and rushed to their weapons. Without rising, Vulic cried to one of the most ardent punters: 'Stake *va-banque*!'[58] – 'I'm on a seven,' replied the latter, running off. In spite of the general commotion, Vulic completed the round; the card came up for the punter.

When he appeared in the line, a fierce exchange of fire was already under way. Vulic was not concerned either with bullets or with Chechen sabres; he was seeking out his fortunate punter.

'The seven came up for you!' he cried, finally catching sight of him in a line of skirmishers who were beginning to force the enemy out of a wood, and, drawing closer, he took out his purse and wallet and handed them over to the fortunate man, despite protests about the payment being out of place. Having completed this unpleasant duty, he rushed forward, drew some soldiers after him, and was extremely coolly exchanging shots with the Chechens until the very end of the fighting.

When Lieutenant Vulic approached the table, everyone fell silent, expecting something original from him.

'Gentlemen!' he said – his voice was calm, although lower in tone than normal – 'Gentlemen, why the empty arguments? You want proofs: I propose to you testing out on oneself whether a man can dispose of his life wilfully, or whether the fateful minute is fixed in advance for each of us... Who'd like to?'

'Not me, not me!' rang out on all sides. 'There's an odd one! What will he think of!...'

'I propose a bet,' I said as a joke.

'What sort of bet?'

'I say there's no predestination,' I said, spilling twenty or so gold pieces out onto the table – all that I had in my pocket.

'Taken,' replied Vulic, in a hollow voice. 'Major, you'll be the judge; here's fifteen gold pieces; you owe me the remaining five, and you'll do me the kindness of adding them to these.'

'Very well,' said the major, 'only I really don't understand what's going on – and how will you decide the argument?…'

Vulic went off in silence into the major's bedroom; we followed him. He went up to the wall on which weapons were hanging, and took down at random one of the variously calibred pistols from its nail. We did not yet understand him; but when he had cocked it and poured some powder into the pan, many cried out involuntarily and seized him by the arms.

'What do you mean to do? Listen, this is madness!' they shouted at him.

'Gentlemen!' he said slowly, freeing his arms: 'Who'd like to pay twenty gold pieces on my behalf?'

All fell silent and stepped back.

Vulic went out into the other room and sat down by the table; everyone followed him. With a gesture he invited us to sit down all around. He was obeyed in silence: at that moment he had acquired a mysterious sort of power over us. I looked him intently in the eye; but he met my searching glance with a calm and unmoving gaze, and his pale lips smiled; yet in spite of his sangfroid, I seemed to read the stamp of death on his pale face. I have observed, and many old warriors have confirmed my observation, that on the face of a man who must die in a few hours' time there is often a strange sort of imprint of inevitable fate, and so it is hard for the accustomed eye to mistake it.

'You're going to die today,' I said to him. He turned towards me quickly, but replied slowly and calmly:

'Maybe, but maybe not…'

Then, addressing the major, he asked if the pistol was loaded. In confusion, the major did not rightly remember.

'Oh, that's enough, Vulic!' somebody cried. 'It's sure to be loaded if it was hanging at the head of the bed; why the need to joke!…'

'A silly joke!' someone else joined in.

'I wager fifty roubles to five the pistol isn't loaded!' cried a third.

New bets were made.

I was tired of this long ceremony. 'Listen.' I said: 'either shoot yourself, or hang the pistol up in its place, and let's go to bed.'

'That makes sense,' exclaimed many, 'let's go to bed.'

'Gentlemen, I beg you not to make a move!' said Vulic, putting the barrel of the pistol to his forehead. Everyone seemed to turn to stone.

'Mr Pechorin,' he added: 'take a card and toss it up.'

I took from the table, I clearly recall, the ace of hearts and tossed it up: everyone's breathing stopped; all eyes, expressing terror and a sort of undefined curiosity, flitted from the pistol to the fateful ace, which, trembling in the air, descended slowly: the moment it touched the table, Vulic pulled the trigger... a misfire!

'Thank God,' cried many: 'it's not loaded...'

'Let's see, though,' said Vulic. He cocked the pistol again, aimed at a cap that was hanging above the window; the shot rang out – smoke filled the room; when it cleared, the cap was taken down – there was a hole right in the middle of it and the ball had lodged deep in the wall.

For three minutes or so no one could say a word; Vulic quite calmly poured my gold pieces into his purse.

Discussion began as to why the pistol had not fired the first time; some claimed the pan was probably dirty, others said in a whisper that the powder had been damp before, and that afterwards Vulic had poured in some fresh; but I said that this latter assumption was false, because I had not taken my eyes off the pistol the whole time.

'You're a lucky gambler!' I said to Vulic...

'For the first time in my life,' he said with a smile of self-satisfaction. 'This is better than faro and stuss.'

'But a little more dangerous.'

'Well, then? Have you started believing in predestination?'

'I do; only I don't understand now why it seemed to me you were sure to die today...'

This same man who had so recently been aiming quite calmly at his own forehead now suddenly flared up and became agitated.

'That's enough, though!' he said, getting up. 'Our bet's over, and your remarks seem to me out of place now...' He picked up his hat and left. This seemed strange to me – and not without reason.

Soon everyone went their different ways home, giving their various views of Vulic's oddities and probably at one in calling me an egotist because I had made a bet with a man who meant to shoot himself; as though he could not have found a convenient opportunity without me!...

I returned home through the empty lanes of the village; the moon, full and red like the glow from a fire, was beginning to appear from behind the jagged skyline of houses; the stars shone calmly in the dark blue vault of the sky, and I found it funny when I recalled that there were once the wisest people who thought the heavenly bodies took an interest in our insignificant arguments over a plot of land or some imaginary rights. And what do we find? Those lamps – lit, as they thought, only to illuminate their battles and triumphs – burn with their former brilliance, whereas *their* passions and hopes have long since died away along with them, like a little fire, lit on the edge of a wood by a carefree drifter! And yet what strength of will they were given by the certainty that the entire sky with its innumerable inhabitants was watching them with interest, mute maybe, but unvarying!... While we, their pitiful descendants, wandering the earth without convictions and pride, without delights and terror, apart from the involuntary fear that grips the heart at the thought of an inevitable end, we are no longer capable of great sacrifices, either for the good of mankind, or even for our own happiness, because we know its impossibility, and we go indifferently from doubt to doubt, as our ancestors hurtled from one delusion to another, without having, unlike them, either hope or even that undefined, albeit genuine delight which is found by a soul in any struggle with men or with fate...

And many other similar deliberations passed through my mind; I did not retain them because I do not like dwelling on some abstract idea or other, and to what does it lead?... In the first flush of youth I was a dreamer; I liked to indulge by turns the images – now gloomy, now cheerful – that my restless and greedy imagination drew for me. But with what did it leave me? Only with tiredness, like after a nocturnal struggle with a ghost, and a dim recollection filled with regrets. In that vain struggle I exhausted both my spiritual fire and the constancy of will essential for real life; I entered into that life having already lived it through mentally, and I began to feel bored and soiled, like a man reading a bad imitation of a book long familiar to him.

That evening's occurrence had made quite a profound impression on me and rattled my nerves. I do not know for sure whether I believe in predestination now or not, but on that evening I believed in it firmly: the evidence had been striking, and despite the fact that I mocked our ancestors and their obliging astrology, I had involuntarily fallen into their furrow; yet I stopped myself on that dangerous path in time and, since I make it a rule to reject nothing definitively and to put my faith in nothing blindly, I cast metaphysics aside and began looking where I was putting my feet. Such a precaution was very opportune: I almost fell over as I stumbled upon something fat and soft, but evidently lifeless. I bent down – the moon was already shining directly onto the road – and what did I find? Before me lay a pig that had been hacked in half with a sabre… I had scarcely had time to make it out before I heard the noise of footsteps: two Cossacks were running out of a lane; one came up to me and asked if I had seen a drunken Cossack who had been chasing after a pig. I announced to them that I had not met with the Cossack and pointed out to them the unfortunate victim of his frenzied courage.

'What a scoundrel!' said the second Cossack: 'Has a skinful of wine, then off he goes, making mincemeat of everything he comes across. Let's go after him, Eremeyich, he needs to be tied up, or else…'

They moved off, while I continued on my way with greater caution and finally reached my quarters safely.

I was staying with an old sergeant whom I liked for his kind nature, but particularly for his pretty daughter, Nastya.

She was waiting for me as usual by the gate, wrapped up in a fur coat; the moon illuminated her sweet little lips that the cold of the night had turned blue. When she recognised me she smiled, but I could not be bothered with her. 'Goodnight, Nastya!' I said as I walked past. She wanted to make some reply, but only sighed.

I closed the door of my room behind me, lit a candle and dropped onto the bed; only on this occasion I was forced to wait longer than usual for sleep. The east was already beginning to grow pale when I nodded off, but it was evidently written in the heavens that I should not get a proper sleep that night. At four o'clock in the morning two fists started banging on my window. I leapt up: what was the matter?... 'Get up, get dressed!' several voices called to me. I dressed in a hurry and went outside. 'Do you know what's happened?' three officers who had come to fetch me said to me in unison; they were deathly pale.

'What?'

'Vulic has been killed.'

I was rooted to the ground.

'Yes, killed!' they continued. 'Come on, quickly.'

'But where to?'

'You'll find out on the way.'

We set off. They told me all that had happened, adding in various remarks regarding the strange predestination that had saved him from certain death half an hour before his death. Vulic had been walking alone down a dark street; the drunken Cossack who had hacked the pig to pieces ran into him and would perhaps have passed by without noticing him if Vulic, stopping suddenly, had not said: 'Who are you looking for, old fellow?' – '*You!*' replied the Cossack, striking him with the sabre, and hacked him apart from the shoulder almost to the heart... The two Cossacks who had met me and were tracking the killer arrived and got the wounded man up, but he was already at his last gasp and said only three words: 'He is right!' I alone understood the dark meaning of those words: they referred to me; I had involuntarily foretold his fate to the poor man; my instinct had not deceived me: I had accurately read on his changed countenance the stamp of his imminent demise.

The killer had locked himself in an empty cottage at the end of the village: we were going there. A large number of women were running in the same direction, crying; at times a belated Cossack would jump out into the street, hurriedly buckling on his dagger, and run on ahead of us. There was a terrible hubbub.

And so finally we arrived; we look: around the cottage, whose doors and shutters are locked from within, stands a crowd. Officers and Cossacks are debating hotly between themselves; women are howling, repeating things over and over again and lamenting. Amongst them I was struck by the eloquent face of an old woman that expressed mad despair. She was sitting on a thick log with her elbows on her knees, supporting her head with her hands: this was the killer's mother. At times her lips moved… was it a prayer she whispered or a curse?

Meanwhile something needed to be decided upon and the criminal seized. Nobody, however, was venturing to rush in first.

I went up to a window and looked through a crack in the shutter: he was pale and lying on the floor, holding a pistol in his right hand; the bloodied sabre lay alongside him. His expressive eyes rolled terribly all around; occasionally he would give a start and grab hold of his head, as if recalling indistinctly the previous day's events. I did not read any great resolution in this restless gaze and told the major he was wrong not to order the Cossacks to break down the door and rush in there, because it was better to do this now rather than later, when he would have come to his senses completely.

At this point an old Cossack captain went up to the door and called him by name; he responded.

'You've sinned, brother Efimych,' said the captain: 'so there's nothing for it, give yourself up!'

'Shan't!' replied the Cossack.

'Show some fear of God! You're not a cursed Chechen, are you, but an honest Christian. So, if your sin has caught up with you, there's nothing for it: you can't escape your fate!'

'I shan't give myself up!' shouted the Cossack threateningly, and the click of the pistol being cocked was heard.

'Hey, ma!' said the captain to the old woman: 'Have a word with your son; maybe he'll listen to you… He's only angering God, you know. And look, the gentlemen here have been waiting two hours now.'

The old woman looked at him intently and shook her head.

'Vasily Petrovich,' said the captain, coming over to the major: 'he won't surrender – I know him; and if we break open the door, he'll kill a lot of our men. Won't you give the order rather to shoot him? There's a wide crack in the shutter.'

At that moment a strange thought flashed through my mind: like Vulic, I took it into my head to test fate.

'Wait,' I said to the major: 'I'll take him alive.' After telling the captain to start a conversation with him and posting three Cossacks by the door, ready to knock it down and rush to my aid at the agreed signal, I walked around the cottage and approached the fateful window: my heart was beating hard.

'Oh, curse you!' shouted the captain: 'Are you mocking us, or something? Or maybe you think we won't manage to deal with you?' He began banging on the door for all he was worth: putting my eye to the crack, I followed the movements of the Cossack, who was not expecting an attack from this side – and suddenly I tore off the shutter and hurled myself through the window headfirst. A shot rang out just above my ear, the ball tore off an epaulette. But the smoke that had filled the room prevented my adversary from finding the sabre lying beside him. I grabbed him by the arms: the Cossacks burst in, and before three minutes had passed the criminal had been tied up and led away under guard. All the people dispersed, the officers congratulated me – and indeed, not without good reason.

After all that, you might think, how could you not become a fatalist? But who knows for sure whether he is convinced of something or not?... And how often do we take a trick of the emotions or a slip of the intellect for a conviction!... I like to doubt everything: this disposition of the mind does not prevent resolution of character; on the contrary, as far as I am concerned, I always go forward more boldly when I do not know what awaits me. After all, nothing can happen worse than death – and death you cannot escape!

On returning to the fort, I told Maxim Maximych all that had happened to me and all I had witnessed, and wished to learn his opinion regarding predestination. At first he did not understand this word, but I explained it the best I could, and then he said with a meaningful shake of the head:

'Yes, sir, right! It's a pretty tricky thing!... Still, those Asiatic cocking-pieces often misfire if they're poorly oiled or if you don't squeeze hard enough with your finger. I must admit, I don't like Circassian rifles either; they just don't suit our kind somehow: the butt's too small – if you don't look out, you get your nose burnt... But on the other hand, their sabres – you've just got to give them credit!'

Then after a little thought he said:

'Yes, shame about that poor chap... What the devil got into him, talking to a drunk in the night!... Still, that was evidently what was written in his stars!...'

I could get nothing more out of him: he is not at all fond of metaphysical discussions.

A Caucasian

Firstly, what exactly is a Caucasian and what kinds of Caucasian are there?

A Caucasian is a creature half Russian, half Asiatic; a penchant for Eastern customs gains the upper hand in him, but he feels ashamed of it in front of outsiders, that is to say, in front of those visiting from Russia. For the most part he is between thirty and forty-five years old; his face is tanned and a little on the pockmarked side; if he is not a staff captain, then he is a major for sure. You find a real Caucasian in the Line; over the mountains in Georgia they have a different tinge; civilian Caucasians are rare: for the most part they are an inept imitation, and if amongst them you meet a *real* one, then it could only be amongst regimental doctors.

A real Caucasian is an amazing man, worthy of every respect and sympathy. Up to the age of eighteen he was educated in a military school and emerged from it an excellent officer; in class he read *A Prisoner in the Caucasus*[1] on the sly and became fired with a passion for the Caucasus. With ten comrades he was dispatched there at public expense with great hopes and a small valise. While still in St Petersburg he had a kaftan made for him, he got hold of a shaggy hat and a Circassian lash for whipping coachmen. After arriving in Stavropol, he paid a high price for a rotten dagger, and for the first few days, until he grew tired of it, he kept it on both day and night. Finally he arrived at his regiment, which was billeted for the winter in some Cossack village, and here he fell well and truly in love with a Cossack girl until the time came to go on expedition; everything's splendid! so much poetry! Then they went on expedition; our young man flung himself everywhere, wherever but a single bullet was whistling. He imagines catching a couple of dozen mountaineers with his bare hands, he dreams of terrible battles, rivers of blood and a general's epaulettes. In his sleep he accomplishes feats of chivalry – a dream, nonsense, the foe is nowhere to be seen, skirmishes are rare, and, to his great sorrow, the mountaineers do not stand up to bayonets, do not give themselves up into captivity, do carry away their dead bodies. In the meantime the heat in summer is gruelling, while in autumn there is slush and cold. Things are boring! Five or six years have flashed by: it's always the same. He acquires experience, becomes coldly courageous and laughs at newcomers who make targets of themselves without need.

Meanwhile, although his chest is covered in crosses, still there are no promotions. He has become gloomy and taciturn; he sits and puffs on a little pipe; in his leisure time he also reads Marlinsky[2] and says it's really good; he no longer puts himself forward to go on expedition: his old wound aches! Cossack girls do not attract him, at one time he dreamt of a captive Circassian girl, but now he has forgotten this all but impossible dream as well. Yet on the other hand a new passion has appeared in him, and it is at this point he becomes a real Caucasian.

This is the way this passion was born: recently he got chummy with a certain friendly Circassian; began visiting him in his mountain village. A stranger to the refinements of the life of society and the town, he came to love a life simple and wild; not knowing the history of Russia and European politics, he conceived a passion for the poetic traditions of a warlike people. He understood completely the ways and customs of the mountaineers, learnt the names of their folk heroes, memorised the genealogies of the main families. He knows which prince is reliable and which a rogue; who is friends with whom and between whom there is bad blood. He has some slight smattering of Tatar; he has acquired a sabre, a genuine *gurda*, a dagger – an old *bazalai*[3], a pistol with decoration from beyond the Kuban, an excellent Crimean rifle which he oils himself, a horse – a pure *shallokh*[4], and an entire Circassian costume which is donned only on important occasions and was made for him as a present by some savage princess. His passion for everything Circassian reaches the improbable. He is prepared to spend the whole day with a dirty local nobleman talking about a rotten horse and a rusty rifle, and is very fond of initiating others into the mysteries of Asiatic customs. He has experienced the most amazing incidents of various kinds, just listen to them. When a newcomer buys weapons or a horse from his local nobleman friend, he only smiles on the sly. This is how he speaks of the mountaineers: 'A good bunch, only they're such Asiatics! The Chechens are a bad lot, it's true, but then the Kabardians are simply splendid fellows; well, among the Shapsugs too there are some tolerable sorts, only they still don't match up to the Kabardians, they can't dress up like them, nor ride on horseback… though they do live cleanly, very cleanly!'

You need to have the prejudice of a Caucasian to find anything clean about a Circassian hut.

Experience of long campaigns has not taught him the inventiveness generally characteristic of army officers; he flaunts his unconcern and his habit of enduring the inconveniences of a military life, he takes only a kettle on his travels, and cabbage soup is rarely boiled up on his campfire. Equally in heat and cold he wears underneath his frock coat a wadded jacket, and on his head a sheepskin hat; he has a strong prejudice in favour of the felt cloak over the greatcoat; the felt cloak is his toga, he drapes himself in it; the rain pours down inside the collar, the wind sets it billowing – never mind! The felt cloak, made famous by Pushkin, Marlinsky and Ermolov's portrait,[5] never leaves his shoulder, he sleeps on it and covers his horse with it; he engages in various sly and crafty tricks to get hold of a genuine cloak from the Andi region, especially a white one with a black trim at the bottom, and then he looks upon others with a certain scorn. According to him, his horse gallops wonderfully well – over a long distance! And that is why he will not want to race you except over fifteen kilometres. Although he finds military service very hard at times, he has made it his rule to praise the Caucasian life; he tells anyone at all that serving in the Caucasus is very pleasant.

But the years fly by, the Caucasian is already forty years old, he wants to go home, and if he is not wounded, this is the action he sometimes takes: during an exchange of fire he puts his head behind a rock, but sticks his legs out *for a pension*; this expression is sanctified by custom there. A beneficent bullet hits him in the leg and he is happy. Retirement with a pension is the outcome; he buys a cart, harnesses a pair of saddle nags to it, and gradually wends his way to his homeland, but he always stops at the posting stations to have a chat with travellers. On meeting him, you immediately divine that he is *real*; even in Voronezh Province he does not take off his dagger or sabre, no matter how they discomfort him. The stationmaster listens to him with respect, and only here does the retired hero allow himself to boast a little, to invent a cock-and-bull story; in the Caucasus he is modest – but after all, who will demonstrate to him in Russia that a horse cannot gallop two hundred kilometres at a stretch, and that no gun will hit the target at eight hundred metres? But alas, for the most part he lays his bones to rest in infidel soil. He rarely marries, and if fate does burden him with a spouse, he tries to transfer to a garrison and ends his days in some fort or other, where his wife protects him from the habit that is so disastrous for a Russian.

Now a couple more words about other Caucasians who are *not real*. The Georgian Caucasian differs from the real one in that he is very fond of Kakhetian wine and wide, baggy silk trousers. The civilian Caucasian rarely arrays himself in Asiatic costume; he is a Caucasian more in spirit than in body: he gets involved in archaeological discoveries, talks about the benefit of trade with the mountaineers, about ways of subduing and educating them. After serving there for a few years, he normally returns to Russia with a promotion and a red nose.

Ashik-Kerib

A Turkish Tale

Long ago in the town of Tifliz[1] there lived a rich Turk; much gold had Allah given him, but dearer to him than gold was his only daughter Mahul-Meheri – beautiful are the stars in the sky, but beyond the stars live the angels, and they are more beautiful yet, and so too was Mahul-Meheri more beautiful than all the girls of Tifliz. Also in Tifliz was poor Ashik-Kerib; the Prophet had given him nothing but a lofty heart and the gift of song; playing on the *saz* (a Turkish balalaika) and glorifying the ancient heroes of Turkestan, he would go to weddings to entertain the rich and fortunate; at one wedding he saw Mahul-Meheri and they fell in love with one another. Poor Ashik-Kerib had little hope of winning her hand, and he became as sad as the sky in winter.

Now one day he lay in a garden beneath a vine and eventually fell asleep; at this time Mahul-Meheri was walking by with her girlfriends, and one of them, seeing the sleeping *ashik* (musician), fell behind and approached him: 'Why do you sleep beneath a vine,' she began to sing, 'arise, madman, your gazelle is passing by'; he awoke – the girl fluttered away like a bird; Mahul-Meheri had heard her song and began to scold her. 'If you knew,' she replied, 'to whom I sang that song, you would thank me: it is your Ashik-Kerib.' – 'Take me to him,' said Mahul-Meheri; and they set off. Seeing his sorrowful face, Mahul-Meheri began to question and comfort him. 'How am I not to be sad,' answered Ashik-Kerib, 'I love you, and you will never be mine.' – 'Ask my father for my hand,' she said, 'and my father will use his own money to celebrate our wedding, and will endow me with so much, there will be sufficient for the two of us.' – 'Very well,' he answered, 'Ayak-Aga, let us suppose, will spare nothing for his daughter; but who knows whether you will not reproach me later on with having nothing and owing everything to you; no, sweet Mahul-Meheri, I have taken a pledge upon my soul: I vow to wander the earth for seven years and to make my fortune, or else perish in distant deserts; if you consent to it, then at the end of that time you will be mine.' She consented, but added that if on the appointed day he did not return, she would become the wife of Kurshud-bek who had long been courting her.

Ashik-Kerib came to his mother, received her blessing for the journey, kissed his little sister, hung his bag over his shoulder, leant upon his wanderer's staff and left the town of Tifliz. And then he is overtaken by a horseman – he looks – it is Kurshud-bek. 'A good journey to you,' cried the *bek*[2] to him, 'wherever you might go, wanderer, I am your comrade'; Ashik was not glad of his comrade, but there was nothing to be done; for a long time they walked together and finally saw a river before them. Neither bridge, nor ford. 'Swim on ahead,' said Kurshud-bek, 'I shall follow behind you.' Ashik threw off his outer clothing and began to swim; on getting across and looking back, there, lo and behold – O woe! O Almighty Allah! Kurshud-bek, taking his clothes, has galloped off to Tifliz, only the dust curled behind him like a snake across the flat field. Galloping into Tifliz, the *bek* takes Ashik-Kerib's clothing to his old mother. 'Your son has drowned in a deep river,' he says, 'here are his clothes.' In inexpressible anguish the mother fell onto the clothes of her beloved son and began to spill hot tears over them; then she picked them up and took them to her intended daughter-in-law, Mahul-Meheri. 'My son has drowned,' she said to her, 'Kurshud-bek has brought his clothes; you are free.' Mahul-Meheri smiled and replied: 'Do not believe it, it is all the invention of Kurshud-bek; before the end of seven years no one shall be my husband.' She took her *saz* down from the wall and calmly began to sing the favourite song of poor Ashik-Kerib.

Meanwhile the wanderer had arrived barefoot and naked in a village; good people had clothed and fed him; in return he sang them wondrous songs; in this way he passed from village to village, from town to town, and his fame spread everywhere. Finally he arrived in Khalaf; as usual, he went up into a coffee house, asked for a *saz* and began to sing. At this time in Khalaf there lived a pasha, a great lover of minstrels; many were brought to him – not one of them was to his liking; his soldiers were exhausted from running around the town; suddenly, passing by the coffee house, they hear an amazing voice; in they go. 'Come with us to the great pasha,' they cried, 'or you answer to us with your head.' – 'I am a free man, a wanderer from the town of Tifliz,' says Ashik-Kerib, 'I shall go if I want, if I don't, I shan't; I sing when I must, and your pasha is not my master.' However, in spite of this, he was seized and taken to the pasha. 'Sing,' said the pasha, and he began to sing. And in this song he celebrated his dear Mahul-Meheri;

and the proud pasha liked this song so much that he kept poor Ashik-Kerib with him. Silver and gold started raining down on him, rich clothes began to shine upon him; Ashik-Kerib began to live happily and merrily and became very rich; whether he forgot his Mahul-Meheri or not I do not know, only the time was running out, the last year was soon to come to an end, yet he was not even preparing for departure. Beautiful Mahul-Meheri began to despair; at this time a certain merchant is setting out from Tifliz with a caravan of forty camels and eighty slaves; she summons the merchant to her and gives him a golden dish. 'You take this dish,' she says, 'and whatever town you come to, display this dish at your stall and announce everywhere that the man who declares himself the owner of my dish and proves it will win it and, in addition, his weight in gold.' The merchant set out, and everywhere fulfilled Mahul-Meheri's commission, but no one declared himself the owner of the golden dish. He had already sold almost all his goods and arrived with the remainder in Khalaf. Everywhere he proclaimed Mahul-Meheri's commission. On hearing it, Ashik-Kerib runs to the caravanserai – and sees the golden dish at the stall of the merchant from Tifliz. 'It is mine,' he said, grasping it with his hand. 'Yours, indeed,' said the merchant, 'I recognise you, Ashik-Kerib; go quickly now to Tifliz, your Mahul-Meheri bade me tell you that the time is running out, and if you are not there on the appointed day, she will marry another.' In despair Ashik-Kerib took his head in his hands: only three days remained until the fateful hour. However, he mounted his steed, took with him a bag of gold coins and galloped off, not sparing the steed; finally the exhausted racer fell lifeless on Mount Arzingan, which lies between Arzinyan and Arzerum. What was he to do: from Arzinyan to Tifliz is a two-month ride, but only two days remained. 'Almighty Allah,' he exclaimed, 'if you do not help me, there is nothing on earth I can do,' and he means to throw himself off from a high crag; suddenly down below he sees a man on a white horse and hears a loud voice: 'Young man, what do you mean to do?' – 'I mean to die,' replied Ashik. 'Just climb down here, if that is so, and I shall kill you.' Ashik descended somehow from the crag. 'Follow me,' said the horseman sternly. 'How can I follow you,' replied Ashik, 'your steed flies like the wind, while I am weighed down by my bag.' – 'True; then hang your bag on my saddle and follow.' Ashik-Kerib fell behind, no matter how he tried to run. 'Why ever do you fall behind?' asked the horseman. 'How on earth can I follow you, your steed is quicker than thought, while I am simply worn out.' – 'True, then mount up behind me on my steed and tell me the whole truth, where do you need to go.' – 'If I could at least get to Arzerum today,' replied Ashik. 'Close your eyes, then'; he closed them. 'Now open them.' Ashik looks: before him are the white walls and the gleaming minarets of Arzrum. 'Pardon me, Aga,' said Ashik, 'I made a mistake, I meant to say I must get to Kars.' – 'Well, what did I say,' replied the horseman, 'I warned you that you should tell me the absolute truth; close your eyes again, then – now open them.' Ashik cannot believe himself – that this is Kars. He fell to his knees and said: 'Pardon me, Aga, your servant Ashik-Kerib is thrice guilty, but you know yourself that if a man has resolved to lie in the morning, he must lie until the end of the day; in reality I must get to Tifliz.' – 'How faithless you are,' said the horseman angrily, 'but there's nothing for it, I forgive you: close your eyes, then. Now open them,' he added, after a minute had passed. Ashik cried out in joy: they were at the gates of Tifliz. Expressing his sincere gratitude and taking his bag from the saddle, Ashik-Kerib said to the horseman: 'Aga, your beneficence is great, of course, but do still more; if I now say I got from Arzinyan to Tifliz in one day, no one will believe me; give me some proof.' – 'Bend down,' he said with a smile, 'and take a clod of earth from beneath the hoof of my steed and put it away next to your bosom; and then if they refuse to believe the truth of your words, bid them bring you a blind woman who has been in that condition now for seven years, rub it on her eyes – and she will see.' Ashik took a lump of earth from beneath the white steed's hoof, but as soon as he raised his head, the horseman and the steed vanished; then he became certain in his soul that his patron was none other than Khaderiliaz (St George).

Only late in the evening did Ashik-Kerib find his house; he knocks at the doors with a trembling hand, saying: '*Ana, ana* (mother), open up: I am a guest from God, I am cold and hungry; I beg, for the sake of your wandering son, let me in.' The weak voice of the old woman answered him: 'The houses of the rich and strong are there for wayfarers to spend the night, and there are weddings in the town now – go there; there you can spend the night in pleasure.' – '*Ana*,' he replied, 'I have no acquaintances here and for that reason repeat my request: for the sake of your wandering son, let me in.' Then his sister says to her mother: 'Mother, I shall get up and open the doors to him.' – 'You good-for-nothing,' replied the old woman, 'you are glad to receive young men and entertain them, for it is now already seven years since tears made me lose my sight.' But her daughter, paying no heed to her reproaches, got up, unlocked the doors and let Ashik-Kerib in: giving the customary greeting, he sat down and with secret disquiet began to look around him: and he sees – on the wall in its dusty case hangs his mellifluous *saz*. And he began asking his mother: 'What hangs on your wall?' – 'You are an inquisitive guest,' she replied, 'it will be quite enough that you will be given a piece of bread and tomorrow sent on your way with a blessing.' – 'I have already told you,' he retorted, 'that you are my own mother, and this is my sister, and for that reason I beg you to explain to me, what is it that hangs on the wall?' – 'It is a *saz*, a *saz*,' replied the old woman angrily, not believing him. 'And what does a *saz* mean?' – 'A *saz* means that people play it and sing songs.' And Ashik-Kerib asks that she permit his sister to take the *saz* down and show him. 'No,' replied the old woman, 'it is the *saz* of my unfortunate son, it is now already seven years that it has hung on the wall and no living person's hand has touched it.' But his sister rose, took the *saz* down from the wall and gave it back to him; then he raised his eyes to heaven and made this prayer: 'O Almighty Allah! If I am to achieve the end I desire, my seven-stringed *saz* will be just as harmonious as on that day when I played it for the last time.' And he struck the copper strings, and the strings spoke out in concordance; and he began to sing: 'I am poor Kerib (a beggar) – and my words are poor; but great Khaderiliyaz helped me descend from a steep crag, although I am poor and poor are my words. Recognise me, Mother, your wanderer.' After this his mother began to sob and asks him: 'What is your name?' – '*Rashid* (brave),' he replied. 'One time speak, another time listen, Rashid,' she said, 'with your speeches you have cut my heart to shreds. Tonight I dreamt that the hair on my head had turned white, but it is now already seven years since I was blinded by tears; tell me, you who have his voice, when will my son come?' And twice she tearfully repeated the request to him. In vain did he name himself as her son, for she did not believe it, and after some time he requests: 'Allow me, Mother, to take the *saz* and go, I have heard there is a wedding near here: my sister will see me there; I shall sing and play, and all that I receive I shall bring here and share with you.' – 'I will not allow it,' replied the old woman, 'since my son has been gone his *saz* has not left the house.' But he began to swear that he would not harm a single string, 'and if so much as one string breaks,' continued Ashik, 'I answer with my property.' The old woman felt his bags and, learning they were filled with coins, let him go; seeing him to a rich house where there was the clamour of a wedding feast, his sister remained by the doors to listen to what would happen.

In this house lived Mahul-Meheri, and on this night she was to become the wife of Kurshud-bek. Kurshud-bek was feasting with his family and friends, while Mahul-Meheri, sitting behind a rich *chapra* (curtain) with her girlfriends, was holding in one hand a goblet of poison and in the other a sharp dagger: she had sworn to die before she would lower her head onto the bed of Kurshud-bek. And from behind the curtain she hears that a stranger had come who said: '*Seliam aleikium*: here you are enjoying yourselves and feasting, so allow me, a poor wanderer, to sit down with you, and in return I shall sing you a song.' – 'Why ever not,' said Kurshud-bek. 'Minstrels and dancers should be admitted here, for here there is a wedding: sing something, then, Ashik (singer), and I shall send you away with a handful of gold.'

Then Kurshud-bek asked him: 'And what is your name, wayfarer?' – 'Shindy Gyorursez (soon you'll learn).' – 'What sort of name is that!' he exclaimed, laughing. 'It's the first time I've heard such a thing!' – 'When my mother was pregnant with me and was in the torment of childbirth, many neighbours came to the doors to ask if God had given her a son or a daughter: they received the reply – *shindy-gyorursez* (soon you'll learn). And so for that reason, when I was born, I was given that name.' After this he took the *saz* and began to sing:

'In the town of Khalaf I drank Egyptian wine, but God gave me wings and I flew here in a day.'

Kurshud-bek's brother, an unintelligent man, drew his dagger, exclaiming: 'You lie; how is it possible to get here from Khalaf in three days?'

'Whatever do you want to kill me for,' said Ashik, 'singers are normally gathered in one place from far and wide; and I am taking nothing from you, believe me or not.'

'Let him continue,' said the groom, and Ashik-Kerib began to sing anew:

'I made my morning prayer in the valley of Arzinyan, my noonday prayer in the town of Arzrum; before the setting of the sun I made my prayer in the town of Kars, and my evening prayer in Tifliz. Allah gave me wings and I flew here; God grant that I become a victim of the white horse, he galloped quickly, like a dancer on a wire, from mountain into gorge, from gorge onto mountain: Maulyam (the Creator) gave Ashik wings, and he flew to Mahul-Meheri's wedding.'

At this point, recognising his voice, Mahul-Meheri threw the poison to one side, and the dagger to the other. 'So this is the way you have observed your vow,' said her girlfriends, 'accordingly you will tonight be the wife of Kurshud-bek.' – 'You have not recognised a voice dear to me, but I have,' replied Mahul-Meheri; and, taking scissors, she cut through the curtain. And when she looked and knew her Ashik-Kerib for sure, she cried out, threw her arms around his neck, and both fell down senseless. Kurshud-bek's brother threw himself upon them with his dagger, intending to stab them both to death, but Kurshud-bek stopped him with the words: 'Calm yourself and know: what is written on a man's brow at his birth, that he cannot escape.'

Recovering her senses, Mahul-Meheri blushed in shame, covered her face with her hands and hid behind the curtain.

'Now it is perfectly clear that you are Ashik-Kerib,' said the groom, 'but tell us how on earth you were able to cover such a great expanse in such a short time?' – 'As proof of the truth,' replied Ashik, 'my sabre will cut through stone, and if I lie, may my neck be finer than a strand of hair; but best of all bring me a blind woman who would not have seen God's earth for seven years now, and I shall restore her sight.' Ashik-Kerib's sister, who had been standing by the door, on hearing this speech ran off to her mother. 'Mother!' she cried, 'it really is my brother, and really is your son, Ashik-Kerib,' and, taking her by the arm, she led the old woman to the wedding feast. Then Ashik took the clod of earth from his bosom, mixed it with water and rubbed it on his mother's eyes with the words: 'All men, know how mighty and great is Khadriliaz,' and his mother recovered her sight. After this no one dared doubt the truth of his words, and Kurshud-bek silently conceded to him the beautiful Mahul-Meheri.

Then in joy Ashik-Kerib said to him: 'Listen, Kurshud-bek, I shall console you: my sister is the equal of your previous bride, I am rich: she will have no less silver and gold; and so, take her unto you – and be just as happy as I with my dear Mahul-Meheri.'

NOTES

A HERO OF OUR TIME

1. Now Tbilisi, the capital of Georgia.

2. Alexandr Petrovich Ermolov (1777–1861) was the commander of Russian troops in the Caucasus from 1816 to 1827.

3. The series of fortifications that marked the furthest limit of the Russian advance through the Caucasus.

4. A fermented beverage made from barley, buckwheat or millet.

5. Friends; see also Lermontov's note on p. 19.

6. 'Beautiful, very beautiful' (Turkic).

7. 'No' (Turkic).

8. A high-quality Caucasian blade named after the craftsman who made it.

9. The song is a variation on the Circassian song in Lermontov's narrative poem *Izmail-Bey* (1832).

10. 'The Russian is bad, bad!' (Turkic).

11. The French diplomat Jean François Gamba (1763–1833) refers to the mountain in his *Voyages dans la Russie méridionale et dans les provinces au-delà du Caucase, faits depuis 1820 jusqu'en 1824* (1825–6), failing to recognise the derivation of its name from the Russian word *krest*, 'cross'.

12. *Cherta* means 'border'; *chert* 'devil'.

13. A monster from Russian folklore which incapacitated travellers with the volume of its whistling.

14. A Caucasian dance.

15. Kizilbech (Kazbich) Sheretlukov continued to lead the Circassian Shapsugs until 1863.

16. The original Figaro was the hero of Pierre de Beaumarchais' comedies *Le Barbier de Séville* [*The Barber of Seville*] (1775) and *La Folle journée, ou le Mariage de Figaro* [*The Marriage of Figaro*] (1784).

17. The heroine of Honoré de Balzac's novel *La Femme de trente ans* (1834).

18. Jean Jacques Rousseau's *Confessions* were composed in the late 1760s, but published only in 1781, three years after his death.

19. 'There isn't one.' (Here and elsewhere the boy uses Ukrainian variants of Russian vocabulary and pronunciation.)

20. 'No.'

21. A distorted version of Isaiah 29: 18.

22. A group of French writers of the 1830s that included Victor Hugo (1802–85), Alfred de Vigny (1797–1863) and Charles Nodier (1780–1844).

23. The enigmatic heroine of Goethe's *Wilhelm Meisters Lehrjahre* (1796).

24. The opening line of Alexander Pushkin's poem 'The Cloud' (1835).

25. While those belonging to prestigious Guards' regiments had eagles on their buttons, members of other army units bore the number of their unit on their epaulettes, buttons and caps.

26. A phrase from St John's Gospel 5: 3.

27. 'Pearl-grey' (French).

28. 'Puce-coloured' (French).

29. The eponymous hero of Daniel Defoe's novel in fact carried an umbrella.

30. 'In the peasant manner' (French).

31. 'My dear fellow, I hate men so as not to despise them, for otherwise life would be too disgusting a farce' (French).

32. 'My dear fellow, I despise women so as not to love them, for otherwise life would be too ridiculous a melodrama' (French).

33. There are differing versions of the story of Endymion in Greek mythology, but he is always the personification of youth and beauty, beloved of Selene, the moon.

34. The evil spirit in return for whose assistance Faust signs away his soul.

35. In his treatise 'On Divination', Marcus Tullius Cicero (106–43 BC) refers to the Roman fortune-tellers' ability to refrain from laughter when looking at one another during their ceremonies.

36. The Ancient Greek scientist and mathematician claimed that the Earth itself could be lifted with a lever, if only a fulcrum could be found.

37. 'Slow fever' (French).

38. A settlement founded by Scottish missionaries in 1802 that was gradually taken over by Germans.

39. 'For a picnic' (French).

40. A variation on a phrase from Act I, Scene vii of Alexander Griboyedov's verse comedy *Woe from Wit* (1825), referring to a mixture of languages, 'The French and the Nizhny Novgorod', i.e. provincial Russian.

41. 'My God, a Circassian!…' (French).

42. 'Have no fear, madam, I am no more dangerous than your cavalier' (French).

43. 'It's priceless!' (French).

44. 'Thank you, sir' (French).

45. 'Allow me…' (French).

46. 'For the mazurka…' (broken French).

47. 'Charming! Delightful!' (French).

48. Pyotr Pavlovich Kaverin (1794–1855) was the subject of poems by Pushkin and is mentioned in the first chapter of *Eugene Onegin* (1823). He served in the same regiment as Lermontov, who would thus have heard many anecdotes about him.

49. The most popular journal of the day, not always noted for the quality of its content.

50. Minor civil servants.

51. A slight misquotation from Act III, Scene iii of Griboyedov's *Woe from Wit*.

52. The concluding lines from the Dedication of Pushkin's *Eugene Onegin*.

53. The reference is to the forest entered by the knight Tancred in Torquato Tasso's *Jerusalem Delivered* (1575).

54. *The Vampyre* by John Polidori (1795–1821), translated into Russian in 1828, was thought at the time to be the work of Lord Byron, and was consequently widely known and appreciated.

55. 'His heart and his fortune' (French).

56. Caesar is reputed to have stumbled on the threshold when entering the Senate on the day of his murder.

57. 'The comedy is over!' (Italian).

58. The invitation is to stake a sum equal to the value of the bank.

A CAUCASIAN

1. Pushkin's narrative poem of 1822, written under the influence of the works of Byron.

2. Alexander Bestuzhev (1797–1837), who wrote under the pseudonym Alexander Marlinsky, was Russia's most popular writer of fiction in the 1830s. Exiled to the Caucasus for his part in the Decembrist uprising of 1825, he wrote a number of works with a highly romanticised Caucasian content.

3. A high-quality Caucasian blade named after the craftsman who made it.

4. A horse from the famous Caucasian stud farm of that name.

5. The cloak figures in Pushkin's *A Prisoner in the Caucasus*, works by Bestuzhev-Marlinsky such as *Ammalat-bek* (1832), and in the portrait of Ermolov by the English artist George Dawe (1781–1829), as well as in a watercolour self-portrait by Lermontov.

ASHIK-KERIB

1. Eccentricities and minor inconsistencies of spelling here and elsewhere in this tale reflect the unedited nature of Lermontov's Russian text.

2. The equivalent of the Turkish bey – a title signifying rank.

Mikhail Yurevich Lermontov was born on 15th October 1814 to a retired army captain and a rich heiress. His mother died when he was two, and from then on he was raised by his grandmother on her estate in the country. There he received an excellent education, and his character was in some ways shaped by the natural beauty of Russian rural life and the exotic landscapes of the Caucasus, where he was taken due to ill health.

In 1827 he moved with his grandmother to Moscow and attended boarding school, where he began to write poetry in the vein of Lord Byron. In 1829 an early verse of his, 'Spring', was published, and shortly afterwards he entered Moscow University, where there was an atmosphere of lively debate on culture and ideology. However, soon after enrolling, he left university due to a clash with a reactionary professor. Instead, he enlisted at the cadet school at St Petersburg. In 1837 he wrote a poem for the recent death of Pushkin which also denounced court aristocracy – for this he was arrested and exiled to the Caucasus. In 1838 he was allowed to return to the capital owing to the petitioning of his grandmother and the influential poet Zhukovsky. It was at this point that Lermontov began to gain popular recognition for his writing, being hailed as Pushkin's successor, and, in 1840, publishing his prose masterpiece, *A Hero of Our Time*.

In February 1840 he was brought to trial for duelling and exiled to the Caucasus again, this time to an infantry regiment for military operations. There he was commended by fellow-officers for bravery. The following year he was given leave, and was returning to his regiment when he was killed in a duel in Pyatigorsk.

Hugh Aplin studied Russian at the University of East Anglia and Voronezh State University, and worked at the Universities of Leeds and St Andrews before taking up his current post as head of Russian at Westminster School, London. His previous translations include Anton Chekhov's *The Story of a Nobody* and *Three Years*, Nikolai Gogol's *The Squabble*, Fyodor Dostoevsky's *Poor People* and *The Double*, Leo Tolstoy's *Hadji Murat*, Ivan Turgenev's *Faust* and Mikhail Bulgakov's *The Fatal Eggs*, all published by Hesperus Press.

SELECTED TITLES FROM HESPERUS PRESS

Author	Title	Foreword writer
Edmondo de Amicis	*Constantinople*	Umberto Eco
Jane Austen	*Lesley Castle*	Zoë Heller
Jane Austen	*Love and Friendship*	Fay Weldon
Honoré de Balzac	*Colonel Chabert*	A.N. Wilson
Charles Baudelaire	*On Wine and Hashish*	Margaret Drabble
Giovanni Boccaccio	*Life of Dante*	A.N. Wilson
Charlotte Brontë	*The Spell*	
Emily Brontë	*Poems of Solitude*	Helen Dunmore
Mikhail Bulgakov	*Fatal Eggs*	Doris Lessing
Mikhail Bulgakov	*The Heart of a Dog*	A.S. Byatt
Giacomo Casanova	*The Duel*	Tim Parks
Miguel de Cervantes	*The Dialogue of the Dogs*	Ben Okri
Geoffrey Chaucer	*The Parliament of Birds*	
Anton Chekhov	*The Story of a Nobody*	Louis de Bernières
Anton Chekhov	*Three Years*	William Fiennes
Wilkie Collins	*The Frozen Deep*	
Joseph Conrad	*Heart of Darkness*	A.N. Wilson
Joseph Conrad	*The Return*	Colm Tóibín
Gabriele D'Annunzio	*The Book of the Virgins*	Tim Parks
Dante Alighieri	*The Divine Comedy: Inferno*	
Dante Alighieri	*New Life*	Louis de Bernières
Daniel Defoe	*The King of Pirates*	Peter Ackroyd
Marquis de Sade	*Incest*	Janet Street-Porter
Charles Dickens	*The Haunted House*	Peter Ackroyd
Charles Dickens	*A House to Let*	
Fyodor Dostoevsky	*The Double*	Jeremy Dyson
Fyodor Dostoevsky	*Poor People*	Charlotte Hobson
Alexandre Dumas	*One Thousand and One Ghosts*	
George Eliot	*Amos Barton*	Matthew Sweet
Henry Fielding	*Jonathan Wild the Great*	Peter Ackroyd

Edgar Allan Poe	*Eureka*	Sir Patrick Moore
Alexander Pope	*The Rape of the Lock* *and A Key to the Lock*	Peter Ackroyd
Antoine-François Prévost	*Manon Lescaut*	Germaine Greer
Marcel Proust	*Pleasures and Days*	A.N. Wilson
Alexander Pushkin	*Dubrovsky*	Patrick Neate
Alexander Pushkin	*Ruslan and Lyudmila*	Colm Tóibín
François Rabelais	*Pantagruel*	Paul Bailey
François Rabelais	*Gargantua*	Paul Bailey
Christina Rossetti	*Commonplace*	Andrew Motion
George Sand	*The Devil's Pool*	Victoria Glendinning
Jean-Paul Sartre	*The Wall*	Justin Cartwright
Friedrich von Schiller	*The Ghost-seer*	Martin Jarvis
Mary Shelley	*Transformation*	
Percy Bysshe Shelley	*Zastrozzi*	Germaine Greer
Stendhal	*Memoirs of an Egotist*	Doris Lessing
Robert Louis Stevenson	*Dr Jekyll and Mr Hyde*	Helen Dunmore
Theodor Storm	*The Lake of the Bees*	Alan Sillitoe
Leo Tolstoy	*The Death of Ivan Ilych*	
Leo Tolstoy	*Hadji Murat*	Colm Tóibín
Ivan Turgenev	*Faust*	Simon Callow
Mark Twain	*The Diary of Adam and Eve*	John Updike
Mark Twain	*Tom Sawyer, Detective*	
Oscar Wilde	*The Portrait of Mr W.H.*	Peter Ackroyd
Virginia Woolf	*Carlyle's House and Other Sketches*	Doris Lessing
Virginia Woolf	*Monday or Tuesday*	Scarlett Thomas
Emile Zola	*For a Night of Love*	A.N. Wilson